THE PANIC WA

[illegible]

[illegible]

[illegible]

[illegible]

[illegible]

[illegible]

Also by Alick Rowe

VOICES OF DANGER

(*Shortlisted for the Carnegie Medal*)

THE PANIC WALL

Alick Rowe

MAMMOTH

First published in Great Britain 1993
by Methuen Children's Books Ltd
Published 1994 by Mammoth
an imprint of Reed Consumer Books Ltd
Michelin House, 81 Fulham Road, London SW3 6RB
and Auckland, Melbourne, Singapore and Toronto

ISBN 0 7497 1772 6

A CIP catalogue record for this title
is available from the British Library

Printed and bound in Great Britain by
Cox & Wyman Ltd, Reading, Berkshire

CONTENTS

Part One
The LION 7

Part Two
The HUT 65

Part Three
The ARK 115

Part Four
The BUNKER 161

PART ONE

The LION

ONE

Gary wished yet again he had not come to the New Year vigil.

'We're going to have fun,' the Reverend Graham Dixon of Saint Barnabas' Church yelled.

Graham was a dickhead and would probably have been called it – even without his surname.

'What are we going to have?'

'Fun!'

'When are we going to have it?'

'Now!'

The boy and girl on stage with Graham rapped out a chord and cymbal clash from synthesizer and drums. There were a few whoops and whistles from the eighty teenagers in the hall. Graham turned back to the microphone. 'Why are we here?'

A joker near the middle called out 'Blackmail!' which earned a laugh but Graham held up his hands for silence. 'We're here at this New Year vigil to forget the differences between us and celebrate what we have in common – which is love and devotion to Our Lord Jesus Christ!'

The biggest cheer of the evening went up. Graham stepped back from the mike and flung out an arm, pointing dramatically. 'We welcome . . . Saint Paul's Methodist Youth Club.'

Synthesizer and drums hammered out a welcome. Simon and his group from Saint Paul's waved as Graham swung the arm towards a corner near the door. 'Statham Street Baptist Youth Club.'

Everyone turned round to clap Betty and her people. They grinned back.

'The Young Peoples' Fellowship from The Hut.'

The YPF were near the hall doors and Gary thought their reception was more dutiful than enthusiastic. A black boy grinned and raised a fist in response but the rest showed no reaction.

Holy Trinity Youth Group were whistling and cheering for themselves even before Graham finished the announcement. The leader, Jackie, was popular. She blew a kiss to Graham who clasped hands to his heart and fell on his knees.

Dickhead, thought Gary. Why did I let him talk me into this?

'And last but definitely not least,' beamed Graham, 'Yours Truly and Saint Barnabas' Sunday Friends!'

More cheering and stomping. More whistling and whooping. Gary blushed and dropped his eyes as attention focused upon his group. When he looked up he found his glance on one of the YPF girls. She was about his own age with very pale skin and dark hair. She was dressed in black. She suddenly caught his gaze and Gary turned hurriedly away to look at his watch. Nine o'clock. There was a lot to do before midnight. Saint Barnabas was the host group and the host group always provided the entertainment. Everyone had to take part.

He looked hopelessly at Graham. 'I can't do it.'

'You'll be fine,' said the man, grinning at the rest of the group for support. All eyes stayed down. Nobody wanted to be offered Gary's part.

'I'm just no good at this sort of thing. I'm not. Honestly I'm not.'

'Try. That's all I ask.' Graham held out a toy telephone. It was plastic and orange. Gary took it with great reluctance. On his way outside he left it on the cloakroom table hoping it might not be there when he came back in.

The new year was arriving on a crisp, starless night. While most of the others scrambled round the tables for sandwiches and soft drinks Gary stood on the stone steps and breathed the frosty air. Several smokers were sitting on the low wall, puffing clouds as they talked and giggled quietly. Gary wandered down the steps and into the car park. He gazed down the road to the pub on the corner, his parents' pub, The Lion. He could hear the customers singing and it sounded as if they were having a really good time. Better than him.

'Gary!' A shape was hurrying towards him across the car park.

'John?'

'How's it going then?'

John was a fellow-student at the Sixth Form College. He came up to Gary, smiling, in his long, black coat.

'All right. There's a break for the food.'

They walked together towards the hall.

'Didn't expect I'd find you here, Gary.'

Gary shrugged. 'I live just down the road.' He didn't mention exactly where. Some Christians disapproved of pubs and he didn't know John all that well yet. 'Who're you with?'

'You know the Young Peoples' Fellowship? We meet at The Hut in Geldorf Avenue.' He laughed. 'The dangerous church! We're charismatics. Who are you here with?'

'Saint Barnabas.'

John laughed again. 'Dickhead Dixon?'

Gary smiled ruefully and nodded.

'Johnny boy!'

In the vestibule they met three of the YPF. They were pleased to see John. A tall girl with spiked hair gave him a hug while the pale girl who had caught Gary's attention earlier slipped an arm round John's waist and kissed him. The boy and John slapped hands. John nodded towards Gary.

'This is Gary,' John said. 'We're up at the Sixth Form College together.'

The black boy smiled and put out his hand. 'Darren.'

Gary and Darren shook hands.

'This is Frankie.'

The girl with spiked hair waved friendly fingers but before John could introduce the pale girl in black, a drumroll sounded inside the hall and Graham's voice boomed through the sound system. 'Lads and lasses . . . if you please . . .'

'See you, Gary,' called John. He and his friends shouldered their way through the doors. The pale girl in black turned briefly back. 'I'm Beth, by the way,' she said.

Instant attraction was something new to Gary. He was cautious by nature and the people he liked had earned his friendship slowly, through familiarity. He watched the door swing shut behind her and found he was holding his breath . . . Beth . . . It was a good name – it was a great name. He pulled himself together and hurried into the hall now more desperate than ever not to make a fool of himself. Graham Dixon had written a short drama about a sinner telephoning God for help and only a dickhead could have an idea as bad as that. Gary was the sinner.

Gary found himself grinning in the spotlight and couldn't stop. Hysteria and stage fright were unsettling him as he waited for the good-natured cheers to stop. The stupid grin kept spreading; it began to tug at the corners of his dry mouth. He felt terrible. He was so scared he could hardly hold the toy phone.

'Hello, Gary,' intoned the girl at the cardboard switchboard in a silly sing-song voice she had not used in rehearsal. 'I'm putting you through now.' The girl fancied herself as a comedienne and overdid the process of finding the right socket for the right plug on the right lead. The laughter encouraged her. She pursed her lips comically and crossed her eyes.

Gary clutched the toy to his ear. It was shaking.

The onlookers saw all of Gary was shaking, shattered with fear. Half the audience felt sorry for him and were anxious that he didn't make a fool of himself. The other half waited impatiently for him to do exactly that. Nothing happened.

'Hello, Gary?'

The cute girl at the switchboard was calling in a baby voice now. 'Is Gary there? Is little Gary listening?'

There was quiet laughter and sniggering. Gary felt Graham's eyes boring into him from the darkness. Mercifully he could see nothing beyond the glare of the spotlight. He forced himself to speak. 'Hello?'

'Oh wonderful!' sang the switchboard girl. 'It's alive!'

There was more laughter and a few whistles. Gary felt stupid and useless. He had known this would happen. Somebody shouted for him to speak up. Gary coughed in panic and heard himself speak. 'Hello? God?' But his breath came in snatches. He could remember nothing about the phone call he was supposed to make to God. He felt as if he might faint, knew he was on the edge of panic, knew that around the edge of the hall four other people from his group were waiting for Gary to give them their cues. His mind was blank and the shaking grew worse.

A deep voice came calmly through the sound system. 'Gary!' it said. 'Good to hear from you. How are things? This is God.'

Reverend Graham Dixon's head swivelled towards the darkened stage where the microphone was. This was not in the script. Gary swallowed nervously. He couldn't see the speaker and didn't recognise the voice. 'Where are you calling from, Gary?'

Silence. Everyone listened.

'Saint Barnabas' vigil,' Gary stuttered.

'So you're at a vigil,' mused God. 'What does "vigil" mean to you, Gary?'

'Being vigilant. Keeping watch.'

'Being on guard?'

'Yes,' said Gary warily.

The voice in the dark went smoothly on. 'What sort of things do people guard, Gary?'

'Valuable things. Money. And criminals.'

Gary stared into the darkness of the stage, the phone still clutched to his ear. He was not shaking any more.

'Don't be vigilant for valuable things, Gary, and don't hang on to your fears. My son came to earth to live among the poor and said you shouldn't even care about tomorrow. Good luck, Gary. I'm always listening. And don't take Dicky's vigil too seriously. It's not worth worrying about. 'Bye.'

Reactions to the divine intervention were mixed. Most people realised something unexpected had happened and the people from The Hut were cheering and whooping. Gary was simply relieved to find the ordeal suddenly over. He was shakily trying to replace the plastic receiver when the phone was ripped from his grasp.

'Hello, God. Still there? This is Graham Dixon on the line.' Graham winked round the hall, grinning like a shark, to let everybody know he was a good sport. Graham didn't enjoy having his thunder stolen and his script hijacked. He was bursting for revenge. There was no response at all. From the direction of the YPF came a low sniggering and slow handclap. Somewhere else in the room someone imitated the peepeepeep of a pay phone waiting for money.

'You're not getting through, Graham.'

Gary recognised John's voice. 'Wrong number, Graham.'

Laughter was spreading through the hall now. Betty switched on the lights and people blinked as they looked towards the microphone to see who had been playing God but the musicians were alone on the stage and Graham thrust the phone back into Gary's hands so hard that the tinny bell jingled madly as he stalked towards the stage to reclaim his show. Gary walked fast to the outside door, needing to be on his own. He had no idea who had stepped in to save him or why. He quickened his steps to avoid the six other members of Graham's group whose entertainment he had ruined. He wondered what would have happened if there had been no intervention and suddenly began shaking again.

'Twelve!'

A ghetto blaster – volume very high – threw the chimes of Big Ben into the totally dark hall.

'Eleven!'

Everyone bellowed the numbers, tired but happy. It had been a good night.

'Ten!'

All round him in the darkness Gary sensed movement and tried to see what was going on.

'Nine!'

People were seeking out their friends in the darkness – friends they wanted to be with at the vital moment. Gary knew the YPF were behind him somewhere, to the right, near the door.

'Eight!'

He began shouldering his way gently through the youngsters around him. 'All right?' an unknown voice asked happily as he passed.

'Seven!'

The doors swung open as somebody entered the hall from the vestibule. The brief glare helped Gary catch sight of Frankie. He pressed on.

'Six!'

Simon's voice roared the number close to his ear, startling him. The leader laughed an apology and patted his arm.

'FIVE!'

There were fewer people round Gary now. He could make out The Hut group.

'FOUR!'

Gary suddenly stopped. Now that he had almost reached the YPF he didn't know what to do. He was surprised to find himself there at all. It was not like him to act on impulse.

'THREE!'

Again the doors swung open – just to his right – and showed him the YPF close by, their arms round each others' waists and shoulders.

'TWO!'

They were in a tight circle, facing inwards, away from Gary and everybody else in the hall. Gary suddenly panicked. They didn't want him. They didn't want anybody. He quickly turned and began to walk to the door.

'ONE!'

Suddenly John had grabbed his arm and was hauling him into The Hut's circle.

'ZERO!'

Every light in the hall snapped on. The spotlight swirled round the company.

'Happy New Year!'

John grabbed him in a swift bear-hug before turning away to Frankie.

'Happy New Year!'

Gary turned to find that the arm round his waist had been Beth's. He gulped.

'Happy New Year!' he agreed.

She kissed his cheek then turned to hug Darren. Gary felt his hand taken firmly.

'Happy New Year, Gary,' said the voice of God. Piers Latham, the YPF leader was smiling at him.

Gary laughed. 'Right,' he said. 'And thanks.'

The hall was a wriggling mass of hugging and hand-shaking. Gary found himself sandwiched between Frankie and Darren as the musicians struck up 'For Auld Lang Syne' and a wavering circle began to form.

'Should auld acquaintance be forgot

And never brought to mind . . .'

Beth and Piers held his crossed hands. He grinned in shy pleasure as they all bawled out the words that almost everybody knew but nobody understood. The chaotic circle began to swing crazily to squeals of happy alarm. A new year. It felt like a new beginning. Gary hoped it would be.

TWO

Gary left the vigil and marched along Church Road, cold hands deep in his anorak pockets. Behind him a motorbike revved up in Saint Barnabas car park and snarled away amid an outbreak of good-nights and happy-new-years. Gary could already see The Lion's car park, empty except for his father's old Maestro. Strange how often you found pubs and churches close together. Not that the two worlds were very comfortable with each other. Gary remembered the all-round embarrassment of the Reverend Dixon's dog-collared visit of welcome to the parish three months ago during opening hours.

Embarrassment . . . It seemed to have been happening all his life. He remembered his mother – a hundred times when he was small. 'Don't take any notice of Gary. Gary's shy. Aren't you, Gary?' He recalled when his father made him join the Cubs. 'Come on, Gary. Don't hide yourself behind the door. We want to see you in your uniform. Don't be daft.' He could still see the grinning men in their Birmingham pub, still feel his cheeks burning and a customer's joke. 'By God, Derek. That's a little Red Indian you've got there, man!'

A van zoomed past him with YPF on its side beneath a dove and a Bible. Beth and John waved frantically, their breath pluming in the frosty air and then they had turned the corner and were a distant grumbling in the next street.

Gary's spirits rose. He was intrigued by the YPF. They were different from any young Christians he had met. It was clear that Graham Dixon didn't approve of them but he was probably jealous of Piers Latham. Gary smiled. The tall leader with the gentle smile had made a right idiot of poor old dickhead and everybody knew it. Gary wondered why John had called The Hut where they worshipped 'the dangerous church'. He wondered if Beth thought it was dangerous. He stamped the cold out of his feet, annoyed with himself at not having the courage to fix up a meeting with her. At that moment the Saint Barnabas clock struck one and Gary came home to The Lion.

'Eyup. Look out. Here he is!'

Harry was wiping tables and emptying ashtrays. He beamed as Gary came in. The bar was still hot and stuffy with cigarette smoke.

'Happy New Year, young man.'

Gary liked Harry. He smiled. 'Happy New Year.'

The Byrnes could never remember if Harry had ever asked if they would appreciate a little extra help after closing-time. The old man had simply assumed that they would. Derek Byrne decided Harry had probably helped his predecessor too and had awkwardly offered him money after the fourth night but it had been smilingly refused.

The door behind the bar counter swung open and Derek barged through, carrying a rattling case of beer bottles. He glanced across to Gary. 'Don't go empty-handed,' he said, seeing the boy heading for the door.

Gary manhandled a crate of empty bottles towards the stockroom. His mother was sweeping the corridor floor. She glanced up briefly and smiled. 'Good party?'

'It was okay, yes. Not bad.'

He could tell how tired she was. Christmas and New Year were good fun but a lot of people had to work hard to make it that way. The midwinter holiday meant long hours, late nights, short tempers and a lot of effort from his parents. The pub must be spotless at all times and – worst of all – every customer expected to be smiled at, listened to, have his troubles shared and his tipsy jokes laughed at. Although the Byrnes were new to The Lion they knew all about the habits of customers and were determined to make a success of it.

The stockroom was a chaos of crates and empty bottles and he looked round to find space. Gary and his father worked side by side, finding the right bottles and slotting them in the right crates – clunk, clunk, clunk, clunk.

'Must have been some people here,' Gary said.

Derek grunted and reached to sling a crate of empties on the top of the nearest stack. For a brief moment he rested his aching back and rubbed his eyes, red and stinging from his customers' tobacco smoke. 'Okay,' he said. 'You finish this lot. I'll work down the cellar. We could have done with you here earlier.'

Gary worked on as he heard his father hurry away. Clunk, clunk, clunk, clunk. Derek always made him feel in the wrong whether there was a reason or not. On the other hand it had obviously been a very busy night and his father had been working non-stop for nine hours. Gary straightened up and lifted the crate on a stack, glad it was only three crates high – he always had trouble with five or six.

'I'm away then, Gary.' Harry was in the doorway, searching the pockets of his old mac for his gloves.

Gary raised a hand. 'See you, Harry.'

The old man grinned and was gone. Gary turned back to the last of the bottles. Nobody knew why Harry preferred to cycle slowly across town to The Lion rather than find a local near his home. It was strange how people could become so attached to pubs. Gary guessed it had something to do with loneliness and belonging. He had no idea how old the man was. It didn't seem to matter. Typical that Harry managed to find the energy for a smile when nobody else could.

A dark splash spurted from a bottle as he flicked it into a case and Gary looked ruefully down at his best jeans and shirt smudged with beer stains and smelling like a brewery. He smiled, wondering what Beth would make of it. Another crate full: good. Gary heaved it up to his thighs, changed grip and hoisted it on to a stack of four as a cycle bell jingled outside. Harry was mounting his stately black sit-up-and-beg bike to begin his journey home. Gary heard his mother call goodnight. Half a crate more and he was finished. He began shifting the bottles faster.

Eileen looked into the stockroom. 'I'm making a pot of tea, Gary.'

'I'll do it if you like,' said Gary. 'I'm finished here.'

She was grateful. 'Thanks, love,' she said. 'I can get on with counting the money.' She took a couple of steps to the door, then turned. 'We're going to press on and get the place ready for opening,' she said apologetically, knowing that Gary was tired too. 'But you're not expected to work. You make the tea and go to bed.'

'That's all right. I'll help.'

She smiled her thanks and moved towards the bar. Gary locked the stockroom and walked slowly along the corridor. Getting The Lion ready for opening meant mopping floors and hoovering carpets, cleaning lavatories, dusting and polishing chairs and tables as well as making sure the shelves behind the counter were fully stocked up. He walked through to the kitchen and filled a kettle, yawning horribly. The clock on the wall showed five minutes past two. They might be in bed in just over an hour if they all kept hard at it.

An hour later Gary sat heavily on his bed and shut his aching eyes. He was dazed with exhaustion but made sure the words to his God were clear in his head. 'Thanks for tonight. It was all right – really good.' He prised off each shoe with the other foot and leaned slowly forward to tug off his socks. 'And thanks for – you know – getting the guy from The Hut to help me out. You know – that orange phone thing.' Forcing himself to his feet Gary hauled his damp and grubby shirt over his head. He unzipped his jeans and let them fall round his feet. 'Thanks for me meeting Beth. Wish I could have talked a lot more with her. Good to have John there too – thanks.'

He walked out of the jeans and flicked them on to a chair. He chucked his shirt on top of them and kicked his socks under the bed. Sliding his shorts off, he reached for the duvet and pulled it up round his shoulders. Then he let himself fall on the bed like a tree, too tired for a shower or pyjamas. He rolled on his side and turned out the bedside lamp. It was getting harder to organise his thoughts. 'Thanks for good business here tonight. And . . . and look after Mum and Dad . . .'

His prayer faltered as it often faltered when his parents came into it. Talking to God about them made him think very exactly what their needs were. This meant Gary had to consider their weaknesses and he found this difficult. After all, they had given up the successful pub in Birmingham to come to a small town for Gary's sake . . . His tiredness solved the problem. Gary felt his thoughts trip and stumble and knew he was being switched off. That was the greatest thing about God. You could always trust Him to know best. He had intended to ask for action on famine in the third world but it would have to wait. He managed a half-awake smile of appreciation. 'Okay then,' he murmured. 'Happy New Year. See you, Lord. Cheers.' And Gary slept.

THREE

On the second Sunday of the new year Gary walked along the road to morning service at Saint Barnabas. The congregation was beginning to gather and inside the church the Reverend Dixon was finishing his customary lap of honour. He had a word with the retired doctor and his wife, smiled at ancient Miss Stanbury and walked over to encourage the organist. He waved to his churchwarden, Colonel LeFort, who was marching outside to chivvy up the late-comers. He glanced at his watch and made his way to the vestry. Time to get dressed up.

When Gary saw Colonel LeFort, spruce, besuited and stern-faced, patrolling the church steps he stopped. Gary gazed up at the huge Victorian building as if he had never seen it before. It was solid, respectable, a hundred years old and seemed to have been specially designed for people like Colonel LeFort to stand guard over. Lost in these new thoughts Gary suddenly realised that the bell was silent and the colonel was turning – swivelling on military heel and toe – About Turn! Then the door was closing behind him and Gary had to rush.

That morning he looked at the service with new eyes, critical for the first time of the half-hearted congregation (of which he was part), the complicated language of prayers, the irrelevance of the Old Testament lesson (which explained in gory detail how to sacrifice pigeons to Jehova) and the boredom of Graham Dixon's sermon which was all about telephones – he gave Gary and the rest of the Sunday Friends an extravagant wink. It was intended to remind them about the New Year vigil but it also seemed to say, 'You and I know this is a waste of time but we've got to play the game. We've got to go through the old, familiar motions because that's the way it's always been done here.' In spite of the size of Saint Barnabas Church Gary felt stifled. He felt he needed fresh air. Ten minutes after the end of the service Gary was racing across town on his bike to the new housing estates. He came to Geldorf Avenue and slowed down. It was obvious why The Hut was so called. There it was – a small wooden building with a corrugated iron roof. It had been built as a church for a small group of worshippers forty years earlier and in recent years had been extended. Now a small covered passage linked it to a pair of Portacabins. Gary leaned on his bike to read the notices on the board. He marvelled at the enthusiastic singing.

'See Him lying on a bed of straw:
A draughty stable with an open door . . .'

Saint Barnabas, like The Lion during the winter months, was nearly always half-empty and its singing quiet and embarrassed. The calypso carol that Gary heard thundering from The Hut was a full-throated roar. And happy too.

'Mary cradling the babe she bore . . .'

Bongo drums pounded out the calypso beat and Gary could hear guitars and a clarinet.

'The Prince of Glory is His name.'

Gary glanced at the bikes chained together. There must have been about twenty. Six motorbikes too. The Hut was popular with young people. He looked at the rows of parked cars either side of the street. The Hut was popular with everyone. The whole-hearted worship intimidated Gary. He did not know exactly why he had come here. It was a complicated impulse – something to do with Colonel LeFort and the Reverend Dixon; something to do with Piers Latham and Beth. But the more he listened, the more he knew he could not be part of what was happening inside The Hut. It was too public. Too . . . embarrassing. He pushed himself away from the notice board and set course for The Lion.

Gary longed to see Beth. He wanted to see John and meet Piers Latham again. Apart from John he had made no friends in the town though this was more of a worry to Gary's parents than to the boy himself. His father was one of a large rough-and-tumble family who could never see any problem in collecting friends. With normal kids, he said, it just happened. When Eileen protested it wasn't so easy for an only child like Gary, Derek was dismissive. 'Of course it's easy. Don't stand up for him, Eileen. He's enough of a mother's boy as it is.'

Gary turned out of Geldorf Avenue and the singing faded behind him. Christmas and New Year had passed quickly and now the holidays were coming to a close. Gary was looking forward to the new term. There seemed to be change in the air. He bent lower over his machine and put on pace for home.

FOUR

The first day of the new term was leisurely. The principal delivered the beginning-of-term pep-talk after which there were two easy sessions – English and economics when nobody was keen to work very hard. The afternoon's drama, with Mrs Bentley, Gary's favourite lecturer, was cancelled to allow students to tour a business exhibition mounted in the hall by the local Chamber of Commerce. Fifteen firms had set up display stands with people to answer questions on career prospects and qualifications.

Gary and John walked round the exhibition together, talking about Graham Dixon's vigil.

'It was really good of Mr Latham to help me out.'

John laughed. 'Piers is like that. He hates Dickhead anyway.'

Neither of them knew what he wanted to do when he left the Sixth Form College but none of the jobs on offer interested them. Gary's parents often brought up the subject of his future so he knew they were concerned. He was concerned too and envious of others in his tutorial group who knew what they wanted to do. Derek and Eileen didn't want Gary to do manual work but office work or teaching had no appeal. He sometimes thought he would like to work abroad but was useless at languages. He was about to ask after Beth when John broke in.

'This is all crap,' said John. 'We're Christians, you and me, Gary. This is all useless.'

Gary was impressed. He forgot about Beth for the time being.

'This is every man for himself. Greed. This isn't what I want to do for the rest of my life.'

Gary knew John's parents owned a farm in Herefordshire and were well off. If the worst came to the worst John could always work with them for a while. The Lion, on the other hand, was owned by a brewery called Bellings to whom Derek Byrne paid rent. It would not be easy to find wages for his son. Not that Gary had ever wanted to work behind the bar counter where shyness would be disastrous. It's all right for you, mate, he thought as they walked to the locker room together to collect their bags. Your parents have obviously got a bob or two. Mine definitely haven't.

The campus was busy as Gary waved John away in his bus to the town centre and strolled towards the bike racks. He swung his bag from one shoulder to the other – it was heavy with new books. Students were everywhere. The Sixth Form College shared the College Hill site with the Art and Technical Colleges and everyone seemed to have ended the first day early.

Gary stopped. At the bike racks two boys about his own age were talking with a girl. He did not recognise any of them. One of the boys was tall and pale; the other was stocky and muscular. All three were laughing. Four textbooks were balanced on the saddle of Gary's bike. Gary did not know why he had stopped and was about to move forward again when the tall boy noticed his hesitation and nodded in his direction. Conversation came to a halt as all three turned to look at him. Gary noticed that the tall boy had steely grey eyes. It was the other who spoke. 'Got a problem?'

The boy wore a military-style camouflage jacket. His hair was cropped short. He raised his chin and squinted at Gary through half-closed eyes.

'My bike.'

They stared at him with blank faces. He felt foolish.

'Bike?'

Gary knew he was blushing. The girl giggled but the boys' hostility felt strong and real. He could not understand why they needed to turn it upon him; he only wanted his bike. The silence stretched until they finally turned away from Gary and continued the conversation as if nothing had happened. Gary hated this. He glanced at his watch, hoping one of them would take the hint. In the end he walked round them and began unlocking his front wheel. They laughed and chattered as if he were invisible. The girl was joking about her computer course tutor. 'He's a right idiot!' She swung the ragged ends of her long woolly scarf and clapped her hands as she laughed loudly. 'No, he is!'

The tall boy began mimicking the new catering manager. She squealed in delight.

Gary straightened up and waited for them to move. He couldn't take the bike even if he steered it away without touching them, the books on the saddle would fall. Suddenly the girl glanced in his direction and their eyes met briefly. Understanding the problem she reached for the books and Gary almost gasped in relief. But the boys stopped talking. The dangerous one laid a forbidding hand on her arm and turned to Gary. 'You want my fist in your face?' he asked casually.

Gary stared at the boy. He felt the blood drain from his face. He felt his breathing suddenly catch and he coughed.

'Push off, git!'

Panic caught Gary in the throat. He picked up his bag and was suddenly walking away, fast, ashamed, scared to look back. He forced himself not to run but it was a small victory.

Gary pushed clumsily through the kitchen door. His father looked up. He was working at his VAT return at the table, a mug of tea near his hand. 'You're late.'

It was a two-mile journey from the campus to The Lion.

'I walked home.'

'Where's your bike?'

Gary prepared to tell as many lies as it took.

'College, Dad. Puncture.' (one)

'Get your puncture kit. I'll take you up in the car.'

'They lock the college.' (two)

'At five o'clock?'

'Honestly (three), Dad. They don't like people there after the last session.' (four)

Gary persisted through five, six and seven, grateful his father's mind was on the complicated lists of figures. He promised the bike was safe (eight, remembering he'd left it unchained) and that it would be good for fitness to walk the journey now and again (nine). No problem (ten). By now he was almost believing his own cover story. Derek had turned back to his paperwork and Gary hurried away, needing the sanctuary of his room.

He was angry. Angry at the boys for having caused the situation and angry with the girl for not stopping it. Most of all he was angry with himself for not being able to deal with it. He slammed himself down on his bed and punched the pillow. Why was it always like this? It was wrong that the bullies, aggressors, idiots, thugs, hooligans – call them what you like – should always win. It wasn't right, wasn't Christian. He wondered what the Christian response should have been. He didn't think turning the other cheek would have been practical or painless. And he'd had to lie. And his bike was at the college, unchained.

He swivelled on to his back and clasped his hands behind his head, angry with God for having let it happen. What was the point of it? 'What were you trying to tell me? What was I supposed to do?' Tears of frustration filled his eyes and he wiped them away angrily. 'This shyness. It isn't just being shy, is it? It's being afraid. I get afraid. I freeze. I panic. Dad would tell me to stick up for myself but I'm a coward. How do other people deal with it, Lord? Does it happen to other people?' He took a deep breath and released it slowly. He had no answer but believed God had heard him and after a while he felt better. After all, nothing had actually happened. He did not know the boys or the girl and since he'd gone four months without seeing them, there was no reason their paths should cross again.

He remembered graffiti on Saint Barnabas notice board. 'The meek shall inherit the earth! . . . if that's all right with everybody else.' He smiled as he swung his legs from the bed and picked up his bag. He started unpacking the books. He could learn from the event, learn to look out for tricky situations and avoid them. What could that girl see in either of those boys? None of it made sense. He wondered if he ought to find another place for his bike but decided that was making too much of it all. He was desperate in case his father saw through his lies and knew him for a coward.

'You're a keen one!' Next morning Gary waited anxiously for the cheerful college caretaker to unlock the gates. It was not yet properly light. There was nobody else about.

'They chuck you out from home?'

'Yeah,' Gary said, forcing himself not to push through.

The man grinned as he swung the gates open. Gary couldn't stop himself any longer. He ran.

His bike was just as he'd left it. Gary almost shouted with relief. He picked up the lock and chained the front wheel to the rack.

'Thanks, Lord,' he said in his head. 'Thanks. Thanks. Thanks.'

After its nervous start Gary's day went well. The first two sessions were with Mrs Bentley and Gary felt particularly at ease with the world as he sat at his table in the dark at the back of the drama room and flicked through the script to check when the next lighting change was due. Gary had tried his hand at almost every non-acting job and found he liked lighting best. Mrs

Bentley was glad as there were always more students demanding to act than help backstage.

'All right, Gary?' she called.

He flicked the stage lights on and off to show he had heard her while Mrs Bentley opened her dog-eared copy of *The Merchant of Venice* which she considered wet-but-worthy. At least it was more fun to stage the plays – no matter how roughly – than endure the boredom of reading them.

After the morning's sessions Gary had lunch with John. Spaghetti bolognese was an unpopular college lunch – not only for the taste the kitchens managed to give it but for the mess it left everybody in. Gary and John stood side by side at the wash-basins trying to get sticky pink stains from their shirts and faces.

'What are you doing Saturday? We're going to Wales. Up in the hills.'

Gary crossed to the towel. It was soaked and he pulled out his handkerchief instead to wipe his mouth. John walked into one of the toilet cubicles and ripped lavatory paper from a roll. He dried his hands.

They moved out into the cold afternoon and began to cross to the main lecture block. Gary's eyes roved anxiously over the crowd of students.

'What's the matter?'

'How do you mean?'

'Who are you looking for?'

Gary took a few steps in silence. Then he grinned. 'Nobody,' he said. 'Nobody at all. Yeah. Right. Saturday sounds great. Thanks.'

Gary's good mood stayed with him through the afternoon sessions of economic history and actually increased when he almost swam a width during his weekly visit to the Vincent Street swimming pool. When he had first come to The Lion he could barely dog-paddle in a small circle.

The Saint Barnabas clock was striking half-past five

when Gary bounced his front wheel over the kerb and rode across the car park to the back-yard gate. It had been a really good day and he felt pleasantly tired. He hung his wet shorts and towel on the line and hauled his bag through the kitchen door. His mother was pouring herself a cup of tea as he came in.

'Good swim?'

Gary nodded. 'Pretty good, yeah.'

'Where did you go? Vincent Road?'

He nodded again.

'I'll pour you a cup, shall I?'

'Thanks.'

'Where's Dad?'

Eileen's mouth tightened briefly as she filled Gary's cup. 'He took his tea into the bar.'

Gary sat and grabbed a sandwich. He was famished. 'Some people are going out in the Welsh hills Saturday,' he said through a mouthful of ham and pickle. 'Is it all right if I go with them?'

He expected his mother to show interest, to ask who the friends were, exactly where they intended going and for how long. 'You'd better talk to your father,' she said as she brought their tea to the table.

Gary was surprised. He glanced carefully at Eileen as she sipped her tea. She looked more tired than usual. She seemed withdrawn. 'Everything okay?' he asked carefully.

His mother looked him straight in the eyes and smiled. 'Fine.' She turned her attention back to her tea. Gary demolished his second sandwich and reached for a piece of cake. He glanced at her again, sensing the atmosphere, knowing something was not right.

Gary found Derek slumped in a chair near the bar fire. On a table at his side stood a plate of sandwiches and an untouched cup of tea. Gary could smell the alcohol as he came close to the sleeping man. Whisky. The only light came from the glowing coals in the grate.

He did not want to disturb Derek but the bar clock showed twenty minutes to opening time and he should be awake. Gary looked at his father; he hated it when he drank too much. It accounted for his mother's mood as they'd probably had a big row about it. At that moment Derek slipped lower in the chair and the jolt woke him. He opened bleary eyes which suddenly jumped into focus at the sight of somebody very close. Then he saw it was Gary and relaxed, straightening himself and rubbing tired eyes. 'What's the time?'

'Twenty to.'

'Twenty to what?'

'Six.'

Derek made an effort to shake off heaviness. He took a sip from the cup but grimaced and immediately put it down. He bit into a sandwich, glancing up to the clock to check the hour.

'Dad?'

Derek turned his reddened eyes on Gary as he chewed.

'Is it all right if I go out on a trip all day Saturday? There's a minibus going from one of the churches. Black Mountains. Is it okay?'

'What d'you want to go up in the hills for this time of year?'

'Just a break. Day out with friends.'

'All right for some.'

His father levered himself from the chair and walked stiffly to the counter for a glass which he filled from the mineral water bottle.

'The church up the road? Dixon?'

'It's a church the other side of town. People from The Hut.'

Derek put the glass down and switched on the bar lights. He threw Gary a sharp look. 'That shed place off Geldorf Avenue?'

Gary was apprehensive. He was surprised his father

had even heard of it. 'One of my friends from college – ' Gary never finished.

'What's wrong with you? Why don't you make ordinary friends? Those people from that shed – they're nutters.'

Gary knew better than to interrupt Derek in this mood. Pubs were great places for gossip and clearly he had picked up a lot of prejudice about The Hut and its worshippers. According to Derek they were do-gooders who encouraged the town layabouts, giving hand-outs to the alkies at the back of the old station. They brainwashed kids. One of Derek's customers knew somebody whose friend's son had got in the clutches of people like that and they'd alienated him totally from family and friends.

'What do they want with you anyway? They're dead against drink. You know that, don't you? Not that that stops them collecting outside pubs on a Friday night. Bloody hypocrites.'

It was a quarter to six. Derek seemed to run out of steam. He stood staring down at the counter. Gary waited.

'You're not asking me or your mother for money?'

'No.'

Derek nodded and waited. There would probably be a last objection.

'There's enough for you to do round here on Saturday without running off to Wales.'

'I'll clean the car before I go if you like. And I could sweep the cellar for you on Sunday – stockroom too.'

Gary picked up the plate and the cup of cold tea. 'I'll bring you a fresh cup.'

He walked towards the door.

'Have you told your mother about this trip?' Derek muttered.

'Yes.'

Gary turned, balancing cup and plate as he twisted the handle. 'So it's all right, is it?'

Derek shrugged as if to say 'What do I care?' Gary saw him filling a small glass from the whisky bottle as the door swung shut behind him.

FIVE

The battered minibus seemed the only moving thing as it threaded its way along the mountain roads of mid-Wales. It was a cold grey day and visibility was good. The only other signs of life were the sheep, as still as statues and as close to the farms as they could get. Some had been missed by the winter gathering and could be seen higher up – small white dots on the vast grey moorland.

The temperature inside the minibus was high with the heater full on and the seven occupants generating warmth of their own as they sang the calypso carol Gary had heard outside The Hut.

'See Him lying on a bed of straw:
A draughty stable with an open door;
Mary cradling the babe she bore –
The Prince of Glory is His name.'

At the wheel Piers sang as loudly as any of them. He glanced in the rear-view mirror and caught Darren's eyes. The boy punched the air and yelled.

'Piers!'

A cheer broke into the singing and Piers grinned as he put his full attention to bringing the bus higher and higher in the hills. The carol's chorus rose above the straining engine.

'O now carry me to Bethlehem
To see the Lord appear to men!
Just as poor was the stable then.
The Prince of Glory when He came.'

They parked where a standing stone dominated a level space, and gusting winds rocked the minibus. Darren and Claire had made sandwiches for everybody and Frankie had brought two large Thermos flasks of soup. The group stood sheltering in the leeway of the bus from the needle-sharp wind and munching in silence like the sheep. At this height there were no buildings, and the immense scale of the bare hills aroused strange feelings. Nobody spoke. It was scary to be in such a remote place where the only concessions to human beings were a rusty waste basket stapled to a standing stone and a crude road twisting up to the mountain pass. A sudden extra-strong blast of wind boomed like a cannon as it hit the side of the bus and snatched a small plastic bag away. It danced above them. They all watched its crazy progress as it swooped, fell and soared straight up, hovered, banked then dived.

Suddenly Darren was after it and everybody was screaming encouragement. He scrambled over the close-cropped grass and swivelled right as a cross breeze flicked the bag left. Darren slipped on his side in a swampy ditch to huge applause but the mad mood was catching. Frankie shrieked off in instant pursuit and John followed her, whooping. Then Claire and Beth were running too and Gary was amazed to find himself a metre behind, shouting as loudly as anyone. Only Piers was left at the bus, calling impossible advice when he could stop laughing and wincing every time anyone fell flat which was frequently.

Then it was all over. The bag hit a patch of dead air and sideslipped lazily into John's hand as he dived full length, skidding a full metre before Frankie crashed on top of him and Claire landed on them both. Darren came screaming happily up to hurl himself on the hysterical pile and Beth was about to follow him when she noticed Gary slow down and stop, grinning broadly but shy about joining the free-for-all. She walked across and they watched the antics together, getting their breath back.

'They're mad,' Gary laughed.

'He says you're mad!' Beth shouted at the wet wriggling mass.

John's face suddenly emerged from an unlikely place in the wriggling heap, streaked with red muddy clay. Clutching the plastic bag, his hand suddenly appeared from somewhere completely different. 'Keep Britain tidy,' he gasped.

Beth and Gary clung to each other, hardly able to stand for laughing.

Piers sipped his soup and watched them with affection. He was a tall man whom women found handsome in a quiet way with his slow smile and gentle eyes but the truth was that he was not a sharer. He was a giver – but only on his terms. This made relationships difficult. He had been Pastor of The Hut for four years and enjoyed the company of the YPF more than any other part of his work. They were all the family he needed and these were the best of the bunch. Moreover, Piers knew that they valued him just as highly. He laughed out loud as the hysterical knot disentangled and, suddenly aware of sodden clothes and arctic wind, began leaping frantically up and down. Piers drained the paper cup and climbed into the bus to start the engine and get the heater working. He peeped the horn to bring them back.

Everybody liked the ruins of Llanthony Abbey under the steep dark slope of the mountain. Strange to think of other Christians of another age at their worship there so long ago.

'Can we climb up to that ridge?'

Even though an hour had passed since the crazy plastic-bag chase and a steamy drive in the bus had dried them out a bit, Piers wasn't sure. The afternoon was advancing and it would be dark sooner than they thought.

'There's a path going up,' said Frankie.

'Please,' said everyone together.

After five minutes Gary looked round for Beth but saw her walking below with Claire. Piers was climbing just behind him and Gary waited for him to come level.

'Did your parents mind you coming?'

'Why should they?'

'We're not popular, that's all. I expect the Reverend Dixon's made his views on The Hut pretty plain.'

The path was uneven and slippery. They trudged upwards for a while. Gary chose his words carefully. 'I don't think he really knows very much about you.'

Piers laughed. 'People like Dickhead sneak up on the Lord in their Sunday best behind big buildings and long words. We don't do that. We walk straight up and say, "Okay, so here we are, Lord". For some reason that frightens people. So they call us dangerous or mindless or nutters.' He sneaked a quick look to see how Gary was reacting. 'You're not afraid of us?'

Gary smiled and shook his head.

They walked past the last of the bare stunted trees. Mist was beginning to wander down from the ridge. Piers put a friendly hand on Gary's shoulder. 'I don't know what God's sent you to us for, Gary, but no doubt he'll let us know.'

The words echoed strongly in Gary. They were exactly what he was beginning to think. It all made sense. The New Year vigil – his rescue from disaster by Piers – finding that John was already part of The Hut – his disenchantment with Saint Barnabas – and now this wonderful day. And also there was Beth. God seemed to have set a great change in motion and Gary had a sudden urge to tell Piers everything about himself – all the thoughts and feelings that added up to Gary Byrne – but at that moment a stream of strange words floated down the hillside and Gary suddenly stopped. Piers laughed at his puzzlement. 'It's Darren.'

They moved on and the high babble of words continued. There seemed to be sentences but nothing made any sense. Gary found it unsettling – even hysterical. 'What language is it?'

Piers noticed his anxiety. 'God's language. Darren's

talking in tongues. You've read about it in your Bible?'

Gary nodded, slowly. 'Just never heard it before.'

Then Frankie's voice joined Darren's. The voices grew louder. The stream of words never faltered.

The pastor explained. 'Claire puts it well. She says it's the Holy Spirit bursting out of you so fast it hasn't got time to make human sense. At The Hut it happens a lot. You just open yourself – you just let go. The Holy Spirit does the rest.'

They were in the fringes of mist now but could make out John and Frankie ahead, resting on a broken-down wall. Darren stood higher up, facing down to the valley with his arms stretched wide. John cheered the new arrivals and the talking in tongues stopped at once. Darren gave a happy whoop and came running down to meet them. He put his hands on Piers' shoulders. 'Great day, pastor,' he said.

Piers grinned and they hugged. 'You scared Gary crazy.'

Darren stepped between them and flung an arm round both. He laughed gleefully as they moved up to flop gratefully on the fallen wall and wait for the others. They gazed down in silence at Llanthony, peaceful and silent below, and the smoke rising to them from the village chimneys. It was a charmed scene and even when Beth and Claire arrived nobody spoke for a long time.

'Okay, folks,' said Piers at last, in a quiet, thoughtful voice. 'Let's go home.'

They came down the hillside in a peaceful silence and where the track widened they automatically hung back or hurried on to form a tight group. John and Frankie put arms round each other. Claire and Darren moved either side of Piers and threaded arms, Beth held out her hand for Gary to take and came close for a calm kiss. The group ambled down to the woodland above the abbey. Gary was totally content. It went beyond sheer happiness. Everything felt exactly right. Beth moved his hand round her waist and slipped her fingers into the back pocket of his jeans. Everything was changing; everything was good.

When Gary got home to The Lion everything was wrong.

SIX

Gary closed the living-room door behind him and moved into the corridor, hearing a burst of noisy laughter from the bar. It was just after nine and he had decided on a shower before coffee. He headed for the stairs, hoping he wouldn't meet any customers in his damp and muddy state.

'Where's your mother?' Derek's face glared at him from the Off-Sales hatch halfway along. His father looked sullen. Gary noticed his words were slurred and was on his guard.

'I don't know. I've only just come in.'

Behind his father Harry was reading the evening paper at the counter and didn't look up. Somebody rapped a coin to draw Derek's attention and his head turned angrily.

'All right all right. I'm coming.' The coin rapped again and his father began to turn unsteadily away. 'Tell your mother I need her down here.' He swayed from the hatch. Gary's dismayed glance focused on Harry who must have heard everything but kept his eyes down.

Gary tapped on the bedroom door and went in. The room was in darkness. 'Mum?'

He switched on the light, worried. Eileen was very upright in her chair at the window, dressed for work, her arms tightly folded. Gary moved cautiously closer. He saw her eyes were red and tired and assumed that was why she had been sitting in the dark. 'Mum? Are you all right?'

'How was your day in the mountains?'

She sensed his anxiety and turned to him, smiling.

Her voice was as tired as her eyes. 'Is it busy down there?'

'Dad says he needs help.' For one terrible moment he thought she was going to cry. The corners of her lips twitched. Or maybe she was wanting to laugh. He really didn't know which. She stood, half-turning from him. 'Pass my cardigan from the bed, Gary.'

He took the light cardigan to her. She pushed her arms swiftly into the sleeves.

'What's the matter with your arm?' He had seen the ugly blue-yellow bruise below her elbow before she could cover it.

'It's nothing,' she said lightly. 'I banged it on the kitchen door.' She turned to face him again and her eyes took in the state of his anorak, jeans and shirt. She laughed. 'Look at you. What have you been up to?'

But Gary was still worried. 'If you don't want to go down,' he said quietly, 'I can help Dad.'

Only the two of them knew the cost to Gary of such an offer. To be young, shy and self-conscious at the counter of a weekend bar was to invite aggravation. There were always customers who wrongly believed alcohol made them witty and considered the person behind the counter a good excuse to prove it. Eileen had always been adamant that Gary should never serve in the bar and even Derek agreed.

'You go and get out of those wet things. Put them by the washing machine. Thanks all the same.'

She turned to check her hair in her dressing-table mirror. 'How was Dad?' Eileen made the question so casual that Gary knew it was important. He shrugged. He didn't know what to say, didn't know what to do, didn't know what was happening. Eileen walked over to the full-length mirror on the wardrobe and smoothed her outfit into shape. She spoke carefully.

'It's always a bad time, isn't it? New year to Easter. Remember last year? Not much coming into the tills but plenty going out for lighting and heat. Your dad gets anxious for the three of us.' She looked at him in the mirror. 'There was a letter from the brewery this morning. They're putting up the rents of all their pubs. That's all.' She smiled as if it was no big deal and checked her image in the glass one last time before moving to the door. She turned. 'You look tired too. Get off to bed whenever you like. We'll manage on our own. Harry will lend a hand after closing.'

'That's all right. I want to help.'

She nodded, smiled and walked swiftly from the room. Gary didn't move. He heard her steps creak down the stairs then the quick clicking of her shoes on the corridor tiles. A customer on his way to the toilets called a greeting and she replied cheerfully. Gary heard the bar door open. A burst of noise rose to him before it shut again.

Trouble. The simple happiness of the hills was clouding. Trouble. Memories of Birmingham. Problems. Gary suddenly felt very heavy and tired. He turned out his parent's light and walked to his own room. He hated it when his father drank too much. It made him surly, unpredictable, aggressive.

Gary worked his frustration off in the stockroom, crating bottles and stacking crates. There was only an hour before the closing-time bell but the bar sounded quiet and dull. People had no money in their pockets for nights out. And the brewery was asking more rent. Gary slammed another full crate into the corner and began to feel better. There was a knock on the door and Harry looked in. 'Eyup, my boy,' he said. 'Heard you working.'

Harry shut the door behind him and sat on a couple of convenient crates. 'You carry on,' he said. 'Nothing I like better than work – so long as it's some other poor bugger doing it.'

Gary smiled as he reached for an empty case and began filling it with empties.

'You don't want to take notice of what your dad

says.' Harry spoke easily. 'He works a long day. He don't mean it.'

Gary slammed the last bottle in. 'Yeah.'

'You don't want to take notice of him when he's on the treacle.'

Gary grinned. In Harry's language 'to be on the treacle' meant to be drinking heavily. Gary lugged the crate up to waist height, changed grip and heaved it on top of the others.

'You have a good sort of time up in the hills?'

Gary suddenly realised he was weary. He took a rest. 'Pretty good.'

'Where you go then?'

'You know Hay-on-Wye?'

Gary ran through the whole day, happy to relive it and relieved at last to find someone who was genuinely interested. He only missed out Beth's special involvement and the weird unsettling language on the Llanthony hillside.

'What's he got against The Hut, Harry? He doesn't know any of them.'

The old man levered himself to his feet. 'You pick up all sorts of gossip in a pub. That Hut – it's got a bad reputation round here. That's all. They don't like the sort of people your friends mix with. They don't like people who show they're different.'

Harry pulled the door open. 'See you later for some clearing up?'

'Yeah. Thanks, Harry.'

The man considered Gary seriously. 'Know where I live?'

Gary shook his head.

'Know Chudleigh Road? On the edge of town? Past the old hospital? Walk up to the end of Chudleigh Road and you'll find me. You will. We'll have a cup of tea one day, eh? Have a chat? You come when you want.'

Gary realised he would like that. It would help. 'Thanks,' he said.

Harry laughed. 'All marriages are up and down, son.'

He was about to close the door behind him when he leaned in again. 'I know mine was.'

He winked and was gone.

Gary stretched his aching muscles under the shower and wished the hot water could wash away his other tensions too. He spoke to God in his head. 'You've got to look after Mum and Dad better. Or if there's something you want me to do, show me what it is. I hate it when it's like this. I don't know what to do.'

Gary turned off the water and stepped from the bath. He tugged the plastic curtain along its rail and fastened it. 'You remember how it was before.' There had been a small incident at the Birmingham pub. Gary didn't know the details but it had been a bad time for Derek and his mother. 'Not that I was much help.'

He had been unhappy at the huge comprehensive, lonely in the hectic pub and miserable everywhere. Derek had told him, man-to-man, that he had been the reason they had left Birmingham. His parents had decided he needed a smaller town and less aggressive surroundings. Gary always felt a great love and feeling of debt for what his parents had given up for him. 'That's why you've got to tell me what I can do to help them, Lord.'

He picked his watch from the shelf and saw it was caked with mud. He soaked his flannel and began to sponge it away. It had been a really good day – apart from the end. He really liked the people from The Hut. More amazingly, they seemed to like him. Beth . . . Beth? Gary looked at the time. Ten past ten. He hoped she would be at the number she had given him and not gone to bed early. He grabbed his towel and padded dripping into his room. This was not like his usual self at all, he thought. It seemed a very good reason for doing it. He dressed quickly and hurried downstairs to phone Beth.

Gary was surprised to find that Beth owned a car. The old Citroën 2CV was neither particularly warm nor comfortable but Gary did not care. They sat in the Saint Barnabas car park watching customers from The Lion straggle home at closing time. It was such a relief to talk to her that he was telling her more than he intended. 'It's not like him. Do you know what I mean? It's the alcohol. He's not like that. Not really.'

Beth said nothing. She knew that Gary needed to talk and guessed he was not the sort of person who would usually open up in this way.

'He drinks when he's worried. That's why a lot of people come to pubs anyway, isn't it? To forget about worries? Only he doesn't forget them and the booze makes him . . . different.'

Gary glanced across to see Beth's reaction but she kept her expression neutral. She wanted him to go on talking. She felt flattered he had chosen her to listen.

'We don't own The Lion, you see. We pay rent – well, my dad does – to Bellings Brewery. They own it. We have to sell their beer but any profit is ours. Only, business is bad just now – very bad. And Bellings are putting the rent up.'

He told her of the bruise he had seen. When he fell silent she reached for his arm and drew it across her shoulders, moving as close as the layout of a 2CV permitted. When Gary found the courage to look at her he found her eyes already on his. She took his head in her hands and gently drew him on to her lips.

Gary closed his eyes in a trance – a genuine enchantment which one wrong move would break. She dragged her lips softly across his then drew back as four noisy men passed the car park and Gary's eyes slowly opened again. In silence they watched the customers' tipsy progress until the most boisterous of the group bade his companions a long loud good-night and turned up a side street. As the three others continued their walk home the clock on Saint Barnabas' tower chimed eleven. Gary cleared his throat. He was finding it difficult to speak. 'I have to go soon,' he rasped. He coughed again. 'Sorry.'

'Listen.' Beth was suddenly speaking in a voice that surprised Gary by its urgency. 'All that – about your dad maybe hurting your mum and the rent and everything – forget it. It's their problem; nothing to do with you. Don't get involved. Right?'

Gary watched two more customers pass in quiet conversation.

'I know what I'm talking about. Adults screw everything up. They get married, settle down and have kids then ruin everything and expect us to be there to pick up the pieces or just be around to get shouted at when they feel the need.'

Gary was impressed – even a bit shocked – at her bitterness. He wondered what experiences could have left her so angry.

'Don't let them spoil what you've got going for you.'

Gary was uneasy. Was this Christian? Did it matter?

'What about Honour Your Father And Your Mother?'

'Honour them as much as you like. It doesn't mean you've got to *like* them. It doesn't mean we've all got to go along with this crazy game of pretending they're perfect.' She suddenly smiled. 'I've got ways of honouring my two that drives them mad.'

They looked at the road through the dirty windscreen and her eyes seemed to soften. Gary had never seen her vulnerable and his heart went out to her.

'How do you know all this, Beth?'

For one moment Gary thought she might tell him but then her eyes hardened. 'That's another story,' she said at last. 'Maybe you'll hear it one day.'

She reached for his head again but Gary moved first. His mouth covered Beth's lips, clumsy and rough. She drew back slightly, murmuring, and the kiss was longer, better, amazing. Gary gasped softly as Beth's tongue flicked between his lips. Gary shifted his position to put his other arm round her but she spluttered and laughed, suddenly turning away to switch on the ignition. The engine coughed and spluttered into action.

Gary sat back in the rattling seat, thrilled and disappointed. He wanted to tell her he loved her but she reached across him and opened his door. 'Out,' she grinned. 'Quick. This could get heavy.'

Gary got out.

'And remember,' Beth called above the engine, 'it's their problem. Stay cool, stay clear.'

Gary nodded, shut the door and stood back as the Citroën turned carefully on to Church Road then drew swiftly away. He followed the lights the length of the road until they wound around the bend leading to the main road.

Gary pulled up the collar of his anorak against the cold and walked briskly towards The Lion. He tried to focus his mind upon his parents' problems but could only think of Beth. It was the first time he had ever felt so drawn towards anybody. He was shocked to find that the only comparison he could find for his feelings towards Beth were his feelings towards God. He worshipped her. He needed her; he longed for her, felt lost without her. He was in love. He wished he knew how she felt about him. Was she agreeing to a relationship? He just didn't know. And at this particular moment he didn't care. The important thing was that he was in love – and Beth must be at least a little in love with him to behave as she did. Mustn't she?

As he came to the back door of The Lion he thought over what she had said about her own parents. He was prepared to consider Beth's tough advice – and even put it into action if necessary – but was relieved to find there was no need. In the bar Harry was sweeping up and Derek was hauling empties into the stockroom while Eileen washed ashtrays. Everything seemed back to normal and with Gary's help everything was cleared up quite soon. The three adults took a quiet whisky to set Harry on his way while Gary climbed wearily to his room, glad that everybody was too tired for argument or emotion.

In the darkness of his room Gary thanked God for the wonderful thing that seemed to have happened to him. He was in love. He wished he could have told Beth but trusted his faith to supply the right words when the right moment came. There was so much to thank the Lord for – Beth, the trip to the mountains, the easier feelings between his parents. He begged God to care especially for Beth and not let her bitterness hurt her. Then, although it was late, he reviewed every moment of the brilliant long day. He prayed for his parents. He thought of Harry. And John. And Piers, Claire, Darren, Frankie. He prayed for everyone except himself. Just before he fell asleep he touched his lips wonderingly where Beth had darted her tongue. He reckoned he had a lot to be thankful for.

Derek came hesitantly into the bedroom. Eileen sat at her dressing-table taking off the last of her make-up. He saw the ugly bruise on his wife's arm. 'All right?' he said lightly.

She shrugged and rose to take her nightgown from under the pillow. He tried to frame an apology. 'Look. About this afternoon . . .' He could not go on. The time for saying sorry had long passed and they both knew it. Too late now. Nine hours of resentment were blocking the way.

'Look I didn't mean . . .' Again his words tailed off. He undid his shirt buttons and pulled it from his waistband.

Eileen turned to face him. 'Touch me once more – or lay one finger on Gary – and you're on your own. You know that, don't you? I'll take him and we'll be gone the same day. You know I never wanted to come here. Just remember that.'

The Saint Barnabas clock began striking one and Eileen drew back the cover and got into bed. Anger and shame swept over Derek. 'Eileen,' he began.

'The subject's closed,' she replied, turning away from him and switching off her light.

EIGHT

The next morning Gary arrived at The Hut just after the service had begun and chained his bike with the others. The singing which had made him nervous before was just as powerful now but this time everything was different. He stopped at the doorway, attacked by last-minute doubts. What if Beth were not there? What if everybody looked at him as he went in? Then he remembered a verse from the Epistle of John: 'Perfect love casts out fear.' He opened the door and walked through.

The Hut was full of people as well as music. Gary edged in and glanced round self-consciously but everyone was too involved with the hymn to notice a newcomer. The first surprise was that the congregation was of all ages – Gary could even see several babies in their parents' arms while at the front there were wheelchairs. A few Sunday suits were on display but mostly people looked smart and casual. Gary was in his Saint Barnabas gear and wished he were as colourfully dressed as most of the other teenagers: a few were spectacular. Gary looked round with more and more amazement. He was not used to this. There was no pulpit or altar as far as he could see. Musicians played from a small platform in the corner and were led by a smiling Darren on his guitar, his eyes closed in concentration. Behind him stood a girl with another guitar, Claire playing a flute and a boy at a keyboard. At their side a young girl in a bright red cap expertly managed a large drum kit. The music drove forward with a fast bouncy beat.

'A new commandment I give unto you,
That you love one another as I have loved you . . .'

A book of hymns, open at the right page, was offered. He took it wordlessly, nodding his thanks. Gary had been too busy taking in his surroundings to notice Piers approaching. Piers laid his hands lightly on Gary's shoulders and looked directly into his eyes. 'Welcome,' he said. His hands tightened and he shut his eyes. Gary knew that he was praying for him. Then the pastor was removing his hands and smiling in his easy way. 'See you later,' he mouthed as he pressed through the worshippers, shaking hands wherever he went. Gary was moved by this reception – unthinkable to be held and prayed for by Graham Dixon. He exchanged a grin with John who was assisting a group of frail worshippers in chairs. Then someone else was pressing through the crowd towards him, singing as she came. Beth paused to kiss his cheek but kept her attention on the hymn and Gary looked down to his book at last, thrilled to have her at his side.

'That you love one another as I have loved you . . .'

Gary was self-conscious about his voice and Beth sang in a confident folk-style which only made him feel worse but nobody was looking at him the way everyone at Saint Barnabas glared at Miss Stanbury when she warbled the high notes. A revelation came to Gary: not only was everybody having a really good time but it seemed entirely the right mood for the occasion. Gary took courage and joined his voice to the rest.

'By this shall all men know that you are my
disciples,
If you have love, one for another.'

Gary felt full of love, had never felt so happy in his life. He thanked God over and over again in his head as his eyes filled with tears. He knew Beth had noticed but she only slipped an arm round his waist and they swayed and sang together.

Gary felt terrible when the service came to an end and he had to leave her. He was expected at The Lion where he always helped to clear up the bars and prepare

Sunday lunch – the only meal of the week the Byrnes were able to share. He had hoped to see Beth later in the afternoon but she and John were busy visiting housebound members of The Hut's congregation. Nevertheless, Gary's restlessness increased to the point where he felt he had to talk to somebody about the wonderful new dimension to his life. He thought Harry might understand other matters on his mind too.

Chudleigh Road was on the very edge of town and Gary slowly cycled its length wondering which was Harry's house. Sunday had continued as blustery and grey as it had begun and it would soon be dark. The houses were closed, curtains pulled and only the blue flicker of television sets betrayed any sign of habitation. At the end of the road Gary dismounted and looked round. This was stupid. The road was a cul-de-sac. Knocking at one of these unfriendly doors for information was out of the question. 'Okay, Lord,' he said in his head. 'Where now?'

Then he saw the path and a battered old sign: 'Allotments'. The path ran along the side of the last house. Gary wasn't sure how helpful God was being but decided to check it out anyway. The allotments were mostly waste ground. Gary could see that once there had been a series of small square gardens but now all except one were derelict. Although it was midwinter the soil of this one patch looked clean and cared for. Alongside stood a long modern caravan whose door suddenly opened to reveal a smiling Harry.

They sat in the snug warmth of the caravan waiting for the tea to brew. Gary looked around as a sharp gust caught the edge of the caravan and rattled the cups in their saucers. Apart from the wind, it was a quiet spot – almost like being out in the country. He looked at Harry's photographs on the wall. One was of a young soldier and a girl – that would be Harry and his wife. The old man edged a cup across the tiny table and saw his interest. 'We had a little house in Purser Street, me and the wife,' he explained. 'Just round the corner from The Lion. But I had one of the allotments here, a nice bit of garden. There were twenty-five allotments then. We used to have a champion time working away in the evenings and the wives and kids would help weekends. Then over the years people stopped coming – well, you could get veg cheap at supermarkets and the time came when I was the only one left; all the other allotments went to seed. Terrible shame. When the wife passed away I thought to myself, well now, where were we happiest? So I sold the house and got planning permission to set down a caravan and here I am fifteen years on. It's nothing now but you should see it in the summer.' He reached for the pot and filled Gary's cup.

'Is that why you come all the way to The Lion every day? Because it used to be your local?'

'It's a place for memories, son,' he said. 'And when you get old, memories really matter.' He lifted his cup and drank. 'Mind you, The Lion was a bit different then.'

'In what way?'

'Busy, for one. Hectic on a Saturday night when the landlady played the piano for a sing-song. All the pubs did good business in those days. Not so much television. Everyone met up at their locals.'

'Now you're our only regular.'

The old man stared thoughtfully into the red mesh of his gas fire. 'Never a good time for pubs: the middle of winter.'

Gary spoke carefully. 'Dad had a letter. From the brewery. They're putting up the rent and going to sell off any pub that can't pay it.'

Harry nodded slowly, his eyes on the fire. Gary felt encouraged to continue. He needed to explain something important to Harry.

'Only – that's why Dad . . . gets on the treacle, I think.'

Harry looked up and saw the boy's worried face.

He nodded briskly in agreement. 'Stands to reason. He's proud of what he's got and what he's done. It's hard to admit things are going wrong.' He shook two more biscuits from the packet. 'Tell me about that pub of yours in Birmingham. Your dad says it did a good trade.'

So Gary told him about The Engineer. It felt a lifetime away, not just a few months, and as he tried to put it into accurate words he realised what a thriving, lively place it must have been and how his parents must have liked it. It made Gary all the more grateful for their sacrifice. He fell silent.

Harry was puzzled. 'Why did you leave it?'

Gary raised his eyes to meet Harry's. 'I wasn't doing well – you know: school and things. Mum and Dad thought I needed a smaller place where – ' Gary shrugged; he had never admitted this to anyone, not even Beth ' – where I could stand up for myself more. Where I'd be happier.'

'Were they right?'

Gary felt a smile creep across his face. Then it became a grin. 'Definitely.'

Harry laughed. 'That's something then. What's made the difference?'

Once Gary began talking about Beth he found he could not stop. He was anxious not to bore or embarrass Harry but the old man clearly enjoyed hearing about her.

'When am I going to see this young lady then?'

'What, bring her here?' It was a great idea. Gary knew Beth and Harry would really take to each other.

'Why not? I enjoy a bit of company.'

'Right. Thanks.' Gary glanced outside. It was dark. 'I'd better be going.' He drained his cup and grabbed a final biscuit. 'I would have brought her this afternoon,' he explained. 'But Sundays are the busiest day for The Hut.'

Harry climbed to his feet as Gary tugged on his anorak.

'I told Beth about the rent going up and Dad's . . . his moods.' Gary instinctively knew it would not be right to tell a customer – even Harry – about the bruise on Eileen's arm. 'She says stay clear and be cool.'

'Maybe she's right, lad. There's not a lot you can do to help matters.'

Gary was ready to go out into the night. He pulled his gloves on and turned to Harry. 'Thanks. I really appreciate . . . you know.'

Harry smiled and nodded. He patted Gary's shoulder. 'I know,' he said. He opened the door. The wild wind surged in, rocking the caravan. The gas fire popped and sputtered in protest. 'You're welcome here any time,' said Harry, 'and when spring comes we might even make a gardener out of you. Why not?'

He retreated inside, waving as he shut the door. Gary lifted his bike, leaned into the wind and made his way towards the distant orange street lights. He had a new respect and affection for Harry. 'Thanks, Lord,' he said aloud. Another friend; another friendly place. He came to the edge of the orange glow and looked at his watch. Two hours before he was to meet Beth at her digs. Time for food, a shower and a quick look at his college homework. The wind knocked him sideways as he swung into the saddle and a sharp scatter of rain stung his face. Gary was having a wonderful day.

NINE

Anxious to see Beth Gary hurried from the newsagent's and made for the bus stop in front of the bank. An icy gust slapped at him, rattling the pages of Beth's magazines. He lugged his school bag across the cobbled part of the town centre towards the group of people huddled in the protection of the bus shelter. Gary ducked into the bank doorway to sort himself out. Tugging off his gloves with his teeth he crouched to unzip his bag and fumble in his anorak pocket for the new puncture repair kit. What a time to get a puncture – not that riding would be much fun in this wind; the bike was better off at home. The cluster in the shelter stirred at the sight of the bus. Gary dropped the kit among his college books and took the magazines from under his arm. From the corner of his eye he saw the bus draw up and straightened swiftly to take the few last steps across the pavement, head down, stuffing magazines in, keen to be out of the wind and on his way to Beth.

'Stupid git!'

Gary crashed into a moving body. Staggering to keep his feet, he slipped, dropped the bag and slammed down heavily on one knee. He looked up shocked.

The stocky dark boy rubbed his shoulder where Gary had collided with him. 'Stupid bloody git!' he repeated.

The tall boy with grey eyes was at his side and both glared down at Gary. People were crowding into the bus now, eager to be out of the cold. Gary climbed stiffly to his feet but neither boy moved. Gary's eyes flicked past them to the bus. He took a step forward and spoke as normally as he could. 'Sorry.'

'You what?'

They would not move and Gary didn't reply because he didn't know what sort of reply was required – only knew that the doors were closing and that a range of faces, amused, interested and indifferent was following the pavement entertainment. Then a jaunty bell rang twice and the faces turned to the front as the vehicle drew away. Now the situation changed entirely. It had made sense until that moment – a boy rushing for the bus, an accidental collision. Without the vehicle everything was different. Gary had no purpose now, was uncertain and vulnerable. That moment had to be redefined and Gary automatically tried to do so. 'I said sorry.'

'*You what?*'

And fear began to chip away at Gary's confidence. It was the senselessness of the question – if it *was* a question. What was the answer? What did it *mean*?

The other boy said nothing. He looked at Gary as if vaguely interested in what he would do next. Gary began to feel helpless. His panic was building a wall round him, closing him in. Gary shivered in the cold.

'I know you.' The stocky boy glared at Gary, still rubbing his shoulder. His friend nodded.

'College,' he confirmed. 'You, me and Tina. Bike, yeah?'

The other remembered. 'Yeah.'

Under the hostile scrutiny Gary's eyes wandered across the street. People were passing. Life was going on. A man and woman, deep in conversation, stepped off the pavement to walk round the three of them without either a glance or pause in their discussion.

The stocky boy suddenly hit Gary in the chest with the heel of his hand and shouted, 'Look at me when I'm talking!'

Gary began to panic and the wall rose higher. His breath began to catch in his throat. He was very scared and they knew it. Gary didn't dare take his eyes from the stocky one but felt the cold, interested gaze of his taller companion locked on his face. Gary coughed, tripped on his breath and suddenly choked. He thought he was going to throw up and fought it. For a few seconds they watched his battle in silence then the dark boy spat on the pavement and began to walk on. His companion lashed out at Gary's bag, kicking it across the pavement. One of the magazines fell out, stuck briefly to the wet pavement then skidded and fluttered away. Gary looked desperately into the grey eyes. The boy was tense, interested in what would happen next. Away to his left Gary heard Beth's magazine flapping against the bank's wall.

'C'mon,' the dark boy called. He had lost interest, had other things to do, but his mate held Gary with his eyes and spoke in a soft casual voice. 'We're going to look out for you. Stay out of our way.'

Then he was walking fast to catch up his friend and Gary was sick in the gutter. People were beginning to gather at the bus shelter again and a group of young children pointed and squealed in delighted horror at his shame and distress. Gary wiped his mouth. His face was burning in embarrassment as he picked up his bag and limped away as quickly as he could.

As soon as Beth saw him she noticed his subdued mood and the sag of his shoulders. They walked in silence up the stairs of the house in Victoria Road that she shared with other members of the YPF. In her room she watched him carefully as she made him coffee. 'You okay?' she asked.

Gary tried to smile but the result only worried Beth more. 'What happened?' she said. 'It's gone seven.' She handed Gary his mug of coffee and sat on the arm of his chair.

'I slipped over. In town.'

Beth glanced at the magazine on her bed. 'What happened to my *Cosmopolitan*?'

Gary briefly rememberd fluttering pages skidding

across a pavement. He thought his hand was going to start shaking and spill the coffee. 'They didn't have it.'

It was a stupid lie. He should not have come. He needed her comfort so much but could not bring himself to confess what had happened. Beth slipped carefully down so that they were wedged together and Gary felt her fingers stroke his hair. He longed to tell her of the absurd event he had just suffered and his ridiculous paralysing cowardice but he couldn't. He remembered how clear and sharp she had been about his parents' problems. He guessed Beth did not enjoy complications and was sure she would hate self-pity. He wished he had gone straight home.

'Want to come for a pizza later? John and Frankie are going.'

'Better get home, fix the puncture.'

She noticed his hand shake slightly as he lifted the mug to his lips and tried to sip. The shaking grew worse. The rim of the mug rattled briefly against Gary's teeth and he coughed. 'Sorry.'

She took the mug from him and put it on her dressing-table. She held the trembling hand. He would not look at her. 'Gary, what's wrong?'

'Nothing. I told you.'

'I care for you,' Beth said. 'You know that, don't you?'

Gary wanted to tell her he loved her, wanted to tell her why he was late, why there was no *Cosmopolitan*, why he needed her so much. Instead he stared straight ahead and nodded. She stroked his hair in silence, watching his face carefully.

There was a knock at the door. 'They must have radar out there,' Beth said in quiet annoyance.

Gary shifted his position as she slid back up to the arm of the chair.

'Come in,' she called.

Piers put his head round the door. 'I smell coffee.'

Beth rose and moved to her crowded table. She unplugged the kettle and carried it from the room for water without a word.

'So how's Gary today?' Piers asked brightly, sitting on Beth's bed and picking up her magazine.

Gary wished with all his heart he felt no need to lie. 'Fine,' he lied. He admired Piers too much to reveal what a feeble wimp he was.

Piers leaned his long body against the wall. 'We were all really happy to see you at The Hut Sunday morning. Enjoy it?'

Gary nodded. He knew Piers sensed something was wrong and dared not look up at the man. He felt the thoughtful eyes resting on him but kept his own head down, staring at the threadbare rug.

'Beth's a lovely person,' said Piers. 'We all love her. We all care for her.'

'I know,' said Gary.

'Good,' smiled Piers and began flicking through the pages.

That night Gary prayed hard. 'Lord, why did you let that happen today? It was really bad. You know that. I need to know why you let it happen. Is it because of Beth? Am I doing something wrong? Please. I just want to understand. Lord, it's nothing to do with leaving Saint Barnabas, is it? Is it Mum and Dad? If there's something I should be doing for them, show me. I only want to know, Lord. Or if this is a punishment, give me some sign what I'm doing wrong. Don't let it happen again. Please.' He tried to pray for Beth and his YPF friends, tried to pray for his parents and Harry. Impossible. Two figures were building the wall – the dark stocky boy and his friend with the steely grey eyes. 'We're going to look out for you. Stay out of our way.'

At the other end of the corridor his parents niggled at each other. Derek had attended a meeting of the local Bellings tenants.

'I want to know what went on. Why won't you tell me?'

'If there was anything worth telling, I'd tell you.'

'I'll find out. You know I will. The others don't keep things from their wives.'

Eileen pulled back the bedclothes on her side of the bed and slid in, grateful for the electric blanket. Derek hung his trousers and jacket in the wardrobe. 'Business is bad,' he murmured.

Eileen reached to turn out her bedside light. 'Have you ever thought why?'

'Time of year. It's the same everywhere.' Derek pulled back the bedclothes on his side and got wearily into bed.

Eileen chose her words carefully. 'Harry was at The King's Arms the other evening – his son drinks there. Harry said they were doing good trade.'

'What are you trying to say?'

'Maybe we'd get some of our customers back if they had somebody prepared to smile and listen to them behind the bar. Somebody who wasn't half-drunk most of the time.' This was dangerous ground and Eileen knew it. Derek said nothing. She felt his tense weight at her side.

Derek switched out his light. It was his turn to choose his words carefully.

'Maybe the guy at The King's Arms gets more support from his family.'

Eileen was scornful.

'I don't mean you,' he added.

Derek was cautious about attacking Gary. 'The church thing. I don't understand it but I've never complained – '

'You'd better not.'

'At least we used to see something of him when he was at Saint Barnabas. At least it was only Sundays and I got some work from him. Since he started mixing with those weirdos from The Hut he doesn't do his share. I never see him.'

Eileen knew he had a point. 'Look, you don't pay him and he's got a full life at the college. It'll be different in the holidays. He's happy. Leave it at that for now.'

'I knew you'd stick up for him.'

'Just remember he's your son too.'

'He's a mother's boy.'

There was no further talk.

The cold water shock punched away his breath and his eyes slammed shut at the first sting of chlorine. Vinegar boiled in his nose. Raw water was clogging his throat then suddenly hitting his lungs. Gary retched and the searing pain in his nose flared up behind his eyes. He thrashed his arms but they were heavy and slow in the water. He tried to kick but sank deeper, twisting and rolling, his feet higher than his head. Panic shattered him. He lost all sense of direction and screamed silently. Water poured into him. He choked in terror as he fought to breathe. He screamed again, knowing he was drowning as Eileen shook him gently awake. He stared wildly round his bedroom and saw Derek sleepy in the doorway. Gary was still screaming quietly as he let himself fall back on his pillow. His mouth closed and he was immediately calm and asleep.

His parents watched him in silence for a moment.

'What was all that about?' murmured Derek.

'Bad dreams,' said Eileen softly.

'I thought we'd seen the last of those.'

Eileen stroked her son's forehead and turned off the lamp. 'You go back to bed,' she said. 'I'll sit with him for a while.'

PART TWO

The HUT

ONE

Gary liked John's funny stories. Alarming and unusual events seemed to happen regularly to him. He was in full flow about a muddled young alcoholic called Sebastian who drank cheap wine at the back of the station and claimed to meet God daily in Safeways when they passed a boisterous group of students clustered round a pile of sporting bags. Popular in the middle stood the stocky boy and his grey-eyed friend. Gary's first reaction was fear. It drenched him like a sudden sweat and he spoke fast in his head to God. Then he pulled himself together. Why should they notice him? And if they did, so what? A bus turned through the college gates and the small crowd picked up the bags and moved to meet it. Gary pretended to be deeply interested in John's story.

'Yo, John!' Cycling towards them was a student from their economics class. 'Yo, Gary!' Still in full flow about Sebastian, John waved.

Anxious not to draw attention to himself, Gary nodded an acknowledgement as their friend wobbled past but he had been noticed. As Gary and John came to the bike racks, a derisive whistle pierced the air. 'Hey! Gary!' Gary kept his head down, pretending not to hear. A mocking voice called, 'Ga-ry!'

John stopped talking and looked towards the group. Gary concentrated on his bike. 'Somebody wants you,' John said.

The coach drew up and the group jostled at the door waiting for it to open. 'Hey – Gary?'

Gary carefully slung his bag on his back, head down, taking no notice. John was puzzled. 'How do you know them? You a fan?' John could see Gary didn't know what he was talking about. 'Football,' he explained. 'That's the Tech College team.'

Gary kept his voice as level as he could. 'The one who was calling – the short one. Do you know him?'

'Eddie Watts. He's the captain.'

'What about the one next to him?'

'Tall, fair guy? Kent Bailey. Striker. Sixth Form College played them at the beginning of the season in a friendly. They murdered us.'

The coach drew smoothly away towards the college gates and Gary and John wheeled the bike after it. In the back window two heads turned briefly to watch them. John raised a friendly hand as it swung into College Road. 'You don't know them then?' he asked.

Gary shrugged.

'Funny. They obviously know you.'

Gary desperately told himself he had nothing to worry about. Nothing at all. He had seen them again. So what? This was a small town. It couldn't be helped.

'You're not listening,' said John.

Gary said he was sorry and listened. They knew his name and where he kept his bike. So what? Forget it. Keep the panic down.

'Gary!' John's voice was sharp with irritation but Gary's mind was blocked by Eddie Watts and Kent Bailey. ('We'll be looking out for you . . .')

'Do you want me to finish this story or not?'

Gary nodded and did his best to listen but all he could think was that they knew where he kept his bike . . .

The next day Gary left the lecture block in a hurry. After half an hour at the Vincent Street Baths he was meeting Beth. He unchained his bike, swung his bag on his back, balanced on a pedal and swung into the saddle and the next moment he was winded and dazed on the concrete. Faces turned at his spectacular fall and found it funny. Gary climbed to his feet. There was a tear in his trousers and his anorak sleeve was ripped. He picked up his bike and saw that the saddle had slipped down to crossbar level. He waggled it experimentally. It was loose – so was the locking nut. He had the choice of walking the bike home for repairs and missing his swim or of riding to the pool with his knees halfway up to his shoulders. Gary decided he had provided enough comedy for one day. At Victoria Street Beth asked why he was late and in such a bad mood.

The following day it was a straightforward flat tyre and Gary remembered his puncture of the week before. He had assumed it was an accident but now he was not so sure. As he pumped it firm he tried to give the impression to passing students that a flat tyre was no big deal but made certain his parents didn't see him wheel the bike into The Lion's back yard for the second day in succession.

And the day after that, Gary took no chances. As he unchained the bike his eyes checked saddle, tyres and pedals. He even gave the saddle an extra twist as he wheeled the machine across the yard, not wanting any secret onlookers to have the satisfaction of seeing him caught out for the third day running. Outside the college he turned into a cul-de-sac for a fuller examination and two minutes later, satisfied, he swung into the saddle. Halfway down College Hill the left lever swung loosely in his grip and Gary realised he had no back brake. He was moving too fast now to drag his shoes on the road and gingerly tried the front brake, hoping it would not lock and swing the back of the bike round or, worse, somersault him over the handlebars. He was moving that fast. Gary kept gently applying it as he hurtled to the junction near the bottom of the hill knowing he could not stop. Gary desperately steered for a narrow gap between the kerb and a white Transit van. He couldn't see any further ahead and just hoped his way would be clear. There was no chance to pray as he rocketed across the junction in a blaze of blaring horns.

A pedestrian on the crossing shouted but Gary had not time to heed anybody's problems but his own. Although the ground was levelling, his speed stayed high and ahead lay the Cromwell Street roundabout which would be packed.

He risked stronger braking on his front wheel but the beginnings of a skid scared him. Gary screamed as a lorry pulled from a side street on his left and he swerved outside it into the middle of the road where oncoming traffic shrieked and twisted out of his path. Fifty metres before the roundabout a road turned off to his left and he knew he had to take it. No opportunity to signal. It looked mercifully empty. As the turn raced up he caught his breath, leaned into the bend and swung left. Centrifugal force began to push him out to the middle of the road. He didn't dare try to turn the handlebars. He saw an oncoming car looming. His mind screamed 'LORD!' as it flashed past. Gary saw the pavement, and knew he would hit it. He hauled the front wheel into the air and lost the last of his control, sideslipping and skidding over the pavement towards a high evergreen hedge. Gary felt a heavy blow to his chest as the hedge cushioned the impact and threw him back to the pavement where he sprawled, shocked and tangled in his bike. He disengaged carefully and eased himself shakily to his feet. The rear wheel was still spinning. The car he had narrowly missed was stationary in the road, the driver staring anxiously back. Gary raised a painful arm to signal he was all right and the car moved off. Gary pulled the bits of hedge from his wet, muddy clothing and hauled his bike upright.

The damage could have been worse. The front wheel was buckled badly and the handlebars were twisted – at least he could fix the handlebars. He repacked his scattered books and saw one of the straps of his bag had snapped. One of his gloves was missing too but he was suddenly too tired to look for it. He wanted to be home. Gary lifted the front wheel and stiffly walked the bike away, still too numb to realise how lucky he had been during the last terrifying few minutes. He glanced guiltily back at the battered hedge. Remembering his manners, he thanked God in his head for any help he had been able to give and decided not to take his bike to college any more. He felt defeated.

'You're not expecting me to shell out for a new wheel, are you?' Derek walked round the bike, shaking his head. Gary was too depressed to argue. Seeing the light on in the yard Eileen came from the kitchen to join them. She took one look at the bike and turned to Gary. 'Are you all right?'

Gary nodded.

Derek found himself taking Gary's side. 'He had a bit of brake trouble on College Hill. No problem.'

They went inside where tea stood ready in the kitchen. Derek was due to open the bar in ten minutes and sipped swiftly at his cup. There was to be a darts match that night and Eileen was making sandwiches for the teams. Gary stood in silence, his bag at his feet. 'The strap on this broke. I lost a glove too.' He walked heavily towards the door. His parents exchanged worried looks. Derek called out. 'Hey!'

His son turned.

'Snap out of it, son. Everybody has accidents. No damage done.'

'Suppose so.'

His mother gave him a searching direct look. 'Is there anything we should know that you're not telling us?'

Gary met her glance angrily. 'No,' he snapped.

Eileen reached for another loaf. Derek knew what Gary was feeling and sympathised, knew how it felt to have things pressing you down. 'I'll give you money for a new wheel.'

Gary and Eileen were each surprised.

'But I'll want some work in exchange, mind.'

Gary nodded, grateful. 'Thanks, Dad,' he said.

The door closed behind him and for a while neither parent said anything. Derek thoughtfully dunked a biscuit in his tea. 'What's up with Gary?' he murmured.

The moment Gary was safe in his room he banged the door shut and began questioning God in his head. 'Why are you doing this? Are you testing me? What for? I don't understand. Everything was going so well. What have I done wrong?' Gary lay back on his bed and closed his eyes. He was aching from the impact with the hedge and his initial gratitude to God was beginning to wear off. 'What have I done to them? I don't even know them. *They* don't know *me*. What's the point of it all? Please tell me. I really need to know. What is it? What's the matter with me?' he asked God as he painfully swung his legs down and padded from the room for a soothing hot shower.

TWO

'What's the matter with Gary lately?' Piers was reading a magazine in his living-room and making the most of a break in the loud music. Beth glanced over.

'Nothing. Why?'

'We don't see so much of him.'

'He's working more at the pub.'

'You're sure nothing's wrong?'

'Why should there be?'

'We care for you both, that's all.'

'Look, Piers. It's between Gary and me, okay?'

Piers read his magazine in silence but a frost seemed to form in the room. Beth was aware of having offended him – and therefore everyone. John spoke from the CD player where he was slotting in a new disc. 'He's moody at college. When I ask if he's got a problem he just clams up.'

Darren was stretched out on the carpet listening to his personal stereo. He took the earphones off. 'Who you talking about?'

'Gary.'

'Go back to sleep,' muttered Beth.

'Piers thinks there's something wrong,' John called down to him.

'What do you think, Darren?' asked Piers.

'Am I my brother's keeper?' Darren smiled and rolled over on his side and looked up at Beth. 'Why don't you ask him if you're so worried? You're the one he fancies.'

Beth was annoyed. It was none of their business. 'I do ask him. He won't talk about it.'

'Then you're not asking him the right way.' Darren

winked horribly and rolled over on his back lifting the earphones of his stereo back into place. His eyes closed and a peaceful smile spread across his face. Then Frankie's new disc rocked into the room bringing all discussion to an end. Piers tried to catch Beth's eye and smile but she stubbornly refused to meet his glance. Nevertheless, as she and Gary were returning to Victoria Road from McDonald's that night she asked him again.

'What the hell's the matter with you lately? We're supposed to be together. Supposed to be sharing things.'

Gary didn't reply. It was a cold February night with a frost taking hold. They crossed an empty street in silence. She squeezed his hand. 'What are you thinking?'

Gary suddenly shook her hand away and swung to face her. His fists clenched. His eyes blazed. For one shocking moment she thought he was going to hit her. She had never seen Gary like this. He tried to speak but his tongue seemed shackled. He shook his head in frustration.

'What?' Beth whispered, alarmed.

Almost immediately the fire in his eyes died and his fists uncurled. Now he looked simply miserable and Beth reached for his hands. 'I don't understand any of this,' she said. 'But when you want to talk, I'll be waiting.'

She leaned forward and pressed her lips against his. They stayed like that for a long time before she eventually stepped back and they turned into Victoria Road where they met Claire and Frankie.

'Hi,' said Frankie. 'How are you, Gary?'

'Fine,' he lied.

THREE

Gary was glad to be at the Vincent Street Baths. Since the incident with his bike, the pool had become even more important to him. It was a haven where he was safe and nobody pestered him with questions that were impossible to answer. Here his only concern was the six underwater strokes he was trying to improve to seven by the end of March, in three weeks' time. Gary splashed through the footbath and alongside the main pool, inhaling the chemical smell, enjoying the deep echoes round him. The attendant was giving tips to a girl in the diving pool. Gary watched her arc gracefully through the air and cut into the water. He smiled to himself. One day. He turned his attention back and stopped dead.

Kent Bailey stood twenty metres ahead, his back to the main pool watching the same dive, hands on hips. The girl who had been with him at the bike sheds was swimming happily in the deep end. There was no sign of Eddie Watts, thank God.

Gary's first reaction was to turn back before Kent Bailey saw him. Perhaps Kent Bailey and the girl would be leaving soon. Perhaps Gary should cross to the diving pool. He could pretend he was watching the diving and would be under the protection of the attendant. Nobody would guess the truth. But another thought steadied his racing mind. The Vincent Street Baths had become his own special place. He valued Vincent Street Baths. They were worth a risk. Hardly believing what he seemed to find himself doing, Gary walked steadily forward. When Kent Bailey turned back from the diving pool he was suddenly aware of Gary before him. Gary took great care to offer no sign of aggression. 'Look,' he said quietly, 'I'm no good in the water. I panic if I go under.'

He was amazed how calm his own voice sounded. Kent's eyes briefly left Gary's face to look beyond him, towards the girl in the pool. They came back to focus on him again.

'I can't swim – not properly swim – so just leave me alone please.'

Kent Bailey considered this seriously. His eyes never left Gary's face. 'We can learn you to swim,' he said at last. He looked again beyond Gary's shoulders. 'Me and Tina,' he explained.

No mockery, no spite. Gary thought he even noticed a smile beginning to tug the corners of Kent Bailey's mouth. He took a chance. 'My name's Gary Byrne.' And he held out his hand.

Kent stared down at it, confused. He looked back into Gary's eyes. 'Gary Byrne?'

'Sixth Form College.' Gary was still scared and alert. 'You play football. You're at the Tech.'

Kent nodded gravely. 'Yeah. Second year.' He took Gary's hand and held it firmly. The small tugging at the corners of his mouth became a full grin. Gary could hardly believe it. He began to smile back. The next moment he was screaming as his arms were pinned from behind and Kent Bailey rushed at him. Locked between his enemies, Gary hit the water and the shock punched his breath away. His mouth flooded and bitter raw water clogged his throat. A searing pain flared up his nose and exploded somewhere behind his eyes. Gary knew he was going to drown.

He found his arms free and thrashed out but his blows were harmless in slow underwater motion. He tried to kick but his knees were pinioned and he was dragged deeper – twisted and rolled in a slow nightmare somersault. Gary screamed silently and fought not to breathe. Hands tugged at his waist. He felt his shorts peeled off and began kicking feebly. Almost at once he was free in air. The hollowness of the pool roared in his blocked ears and he thrashed towards the rail where he clung sobbing and snorting as his lungs were racked with coughing and peppery water streamed from his nose. His head throbbed. His eyes stung. Somebody was shouting. He stared frantically up.

'What's going on?' The attendant was crouched above him. 'You know the rules. No fooling about.' The attendant was angry. He could see that Gary had not caused his own distress and knew he should have been supervising the main pool instead of showing off to the girls. The man glared round but could see no one to blame. He looked back down at Gary. 'Somebody have a go at you?'

Gary shook his head very slowly and the man straightened up, unable to take the matter further. He began a keen-eyed circuit of the pool letting everybody know he was there. Gary clung shivering to the rail, incapable of moving.

When the man had passed them, Eddie drew Gary's shorts from the water and flourished them triumphantly. There was a scream of laughter from a group of children who eagerly scanned the pool in search of the unfortunate owner.

Tina was not laughing. 'Give,' she said, holding out a hand.

Eddie floated idly for a moment. He didn't like being told what to do, even by his girlfriend. In a great flurry and scatter of water, Kent shot to the surface at his side.

'I said give, Eddie.'

Eddie tossed the shorts dismissively at her and swam away with Kent in an elegant crawl. At the side they hauled themselves from the water, ran across to the diving pool and launched themselves in spectacular racing dives.

Tina swam across to Gary shaking at the rail. He

wouldn't look at her and seemed unable to speak. She wondered if she should call the attendant but that would mean getting on the wrong side of Eddie. In any case, the boy was big enough to look after himself. She draped the shorts over his tight white fingers. 'Look,' she said. 'You've got to stand up to them or they'll walk all over you. They will.'

Gary was very cold and his teeth began chattering loudly. He kept his eyes fixed on the tiles six inches from his face.

'Get these on and put yourself under a hot shower. Right?'

Gary managed to nod. Tina kicked away from the side and swam back towards the steps.

Gary focused every bit of his concentration on unfastening his left hand from the rail and taking a grip on his shorts. As the squealing children splashed towards him he began the long clumsy journey along the rail to the shallow end. A grinning boy duck-dived close to Gary, spluttering gleefully back to the surface and yelling for his friends to do the same. Gary was hardly aware of them. He centred all his willpower in moving hand to hand along the rail to a depth where he was able to stand and force himself to let go. It took him a long time to balance and pull on his shorts before climbing shakily from the water. He walked towards the showers, trying to keep his eyes straight ahead as he came near the diving pool.

But he couldn't help seeing Eddie and Kent. They were on the highest board about to dive. He saw them laughing, counting down. He saw them begin their run and then – at the very edge – Eddie nudged Kent off balance and Kent shouted as he toppled from the board, managing to fold himself into a passable dive before he hit the water. Eddie followed gracefully, stretching through the air to slice the surface with barely a ripple.

Gary knew he would never dive from any of the boards. It was just a daydream. He would never swim his width underwater. He walked through the door into the showers. This would be his last visit to the Vincent Street Baths.

FOUR

They sat in the warm caravan while Gary poured out his problem and Harry just let the boy speak. Gary told the entire story – from the moment he had noticed books on his saddle until his ordeal two hours ago. When he finished there was silence except for the wind gusting outside and the comforting hiss of the gas fire.

'Have you told your mum and dad any of this?'

They were not to know. Gary was definite. They had left a good business in Birmingham for The Lion because of him – Harry already knew this. How could Gary tell them he was letting them down again?

'Anyway,' Gary murmured, 'they've got troubles of their own.'

'The rent, you mean?'

It was part of what he meant. Gary nodded.

'What about your young lady?'

But Gary didn't want Beth involved. He was honest. He told Harry that he feared she would finish the friendship if it got complicated. Anyway he would feel stupid telling her he couldn't handle his own problems.

'Nobody else from The Hut you could talk to?'

Gary shook his head.

'Well now, my boy,' Harry said. 'Seems to me you've got a pretty low opinion of yourself but you can't be such a bad chap if you've got friends like you have. Your mum and dad – they're proud of you. Why not? You're a clever lad at college. Yet here you are letting a couple of yobbos spoil everything. It's nothing personal to them, you know – if it wasn't you it'd be somebody else. You're even doing their job for them, putting yourself down like this.'

It made sense. Gary nodded slowly. 'What should I do then, Harry?'

'Keep out of their way. That's not being a coward – it's common sense. They'll forget all about you in time. I came across enough bullying in the army to last me a lifetime and I know what I'm talking about, believe me.' He opened a packet of chocolate biscuits and shook a couple on to the table. They munched in silence for a while. 'These yobbos – you don't want to tell me their names?'

Gary shook his head and listened to the wind rushing through the bare branches. To give their names to Harry would make them sharper, stronger, more important. And he was afraid that somehow – he didn't know how – they might find out.

'This swimming, Gary. It's important to you?'

'It was. I can't go back.'

'But you say this was the first time you'd seen them there.'

'They'll look for me there again. I know they will. Do you know what it's like to be scared, Harry? Really scared?'

Harry shut his eyes briefly. On the screen of his mind he saw the beaches at Dunkirk – himself in the sea up to his chest waiting to be rescued – waves slopping into his face and enemy fighters overhead. He opened his eyes. 'I expect so.'

'Then you understand. I'm just useless. I go to pieces. I can't do anything.'

'You did something this afternoon. It was brave to speak to the tall lad.'

Gary smiled ruefully. 'Yeah. And look where it got me.' He stood and reached for his anorak and scarf. Another good thing about a caravan – everything close to hand. He was not keen to leave. He felt safe and secure in the caravan with Harry. 'I've got to go now,' he said reluctantly. 'Thanks for listening. And for the advice.'

'Don't give up your swimming. Or your bike. Don't let them win, Gary lad.'

'They *have* won.'

'Rubbish. They've scared you a couple of times, that's all. Why not? They'd scare *me*. They won't win the war until you wave the white flag.'

The old man climbed stiffly from his chair as Gary wrapped up against the March winds.

'Suppose so.'

Harry waited at the door. He looked pleased with himself. 'I may be able to do something about this,' he said.

Gary was wary.

'What?'

'Never you mind.'

Gary was ready to go. He knew he could trust Harry. He smiled. 'Thanks again, Harry. You know – for the biscuits. And everything.'

Harry opened the door and the boy went out into the night. Harry firmly shut out the cold and turned to light the flame under his kettle. Poor boy, he thought as he sank heavily back into the armchair from Purser Street. He looked up to the picture of his wife. 'Poor boy,' he said to her. 'We'll have to do what we can. Why not?'

But for a while it seemed that Harry was right and Gary's fears were groundless. The very next morning, for instance, Gary almost walked into Eddie and Kent as he got off the bus outside the college. They hurried towards the gates in deep conversation with Tina. Gary felt the quick bite of fear in the pit of his stomach and the familiar flood of helplessness but the three were oblivious to everybody else as they passed. He looked out for them during the rest of the day but they did not appear again.

'When are you getting your bike back?' asked John

as they walked into the economics room.

'When I've got the cash together,' Gary lied.

'Why don't I come swimming with you next week?' John asked.

'Too much work,' lied Gary.

'What work?'

Gary was grateful to be able to tell John something that was true, for a change. 'Mrs Bentley and *The Merchant of* bloody *Venice*.'

Gary had another chance to talk privately with Harry as they helped clear up The Lion on Saturday night but the man behaved as if their conversation in the caravan had never taken place and Gary was secretly relieved. The problem was solving itself and he was beginning to agree that he had made too much of it. Derek heard Harry's ancient bike rattle into the night as he carried a crate of cider to the bar. He glanced at Gary who was checking that the windows were locked. 'Harry's away then?'

'Yeah. He said good-night.'

Derek grunted as he began to stack the bottles on their shelf. 'I suppose you're out with your nutty mates tomorrow morning?'

Gary riddled the fire and put the guard in place. 'Not necessarily.'

Derek was surprised. He continued carefully. 'Only, if you want to earn something towards that wheel, the inside of all these windows could do with a clean.'

Gary looked at them as he pulled the curtains shut. It was the cigarette smoke that did it. They had to be washed every few weeks. 'All right.'

'And what about the glass shelves and mirrors while you're at it?'

'If you like.'

Derek grunted, pleased, and left the bar to connect a new barrel to the beer pumps. Gary slid the security bolts across the front door. He would miss the morning service at The Hut and yet the truth was that he would feel ill at ease there. The YPF continually proclaimed that their behaviour was based on love and straightforwardness. They were right. It showed in their lives. They were open and honest, full of goodwill and charity. Yet Gary could only answer with deception and secret fears. He was embarrassed by their love. He didn't feel worthy of it. Gary checked the dying fire and hooked the guard in place. He thought Harry had not mentioned the problem tonight because he wanted to show it was not so important. Clever.

FIVE

It took Gary most of Sunday morning to wash the foul-smelling tar from the windows and polish the mirrors and glass shelves. He was idly spraying the final mirror in the ladies' toilets when he heard his mother unlock the front door and call a welcome to the first customers which encouraged him to complete the job in record time.

The Saint Barnabas clock struck as he was hanging out the wet cloths in the back yard, reminding him that this was the first Sunday for a long time in which he hadn't been to a morning service. He hoped God would understand that today he needed time out. In the kitchen he laid the table for lunch – the only meal of the week the Byrnes were able to eat together. It would be three o'clock before that happened and Gary was snacking on cheese and crisps when Eileen came from the bar with a smile. 'All right?'

'Great.'

She opened the oven to check on the progress of the chicken and adjusted the heat. 'You did a good job on the windows.'

'Yeah. I washed the cloths.'

'We're grateful, love. Coming in for a chat with Harry? It's quiet in the bar at the moment.'

'Better do some economics.'

She gave him another smile and hurried back to work. Gary switched on the kettle for a coffee. Slowly but surely his spirits were rising. He'd enjoyed working with his mother and father – there was something right about it. He would be glad of the cash too. He glanced out at the cloths tugging at the line. The wind had lost its icy edge today. Maybe winter was over at last. He looked at the kitchen clock as he left and wondered what Beth was doing.

Beth was arriving back at Victoria Road where she had digs with Mr and Mrs Turner. Mr and Mrs T were well respected at The Hut as the last survivors of the group who broke away from Saint Martin's Church in 1950 to find a simpler style of worship. Within a year they had raised enough money to buy a patch of land and when the group appointed its first pastor Mr and Mrs Turner offered him a free self-contained flat at their home.

Piers was the fourth pastor to have lived at 180 Victoria Road and it was he who suggested that the flat should become a meeting-place for young people of the Fellowship he had just formed. It was lucky that Mr Turner was a sympathetic – as well as fit and healthy – retired builder with time on his hands. He built a downstairs flat for his wife and himself after which he converted the remaining upstairs rooms into three bedsits and a bathroom. The Turners never asked for rent – though Piers insisted everyone in the house should hand him an appropriate sum each week which he put into a Building Society account for repairs and emergencies. Mr and Mrs Turner never mentioned this fund although they were occasionally forced to dip into it.

Because of its reputation for giving refuge to a variety of young people 180 Victoria Road became known to The Hut as 'The Ark'. Mr and Mrs T liked the name. They liked the arrangement. 'It keeps you young,' they told friends who asked how they managed to put up with the noise. Beth was their latest refugee.

'So where was your little friend this morning?' Claire asked as they shut the front door behind them.

'Only us, Mrs T,' they chorused to their unseen landlady as they hurried towards the stairs, glad to be out of the wind.

'No Gary today,' said John, upstairs, pouring cider for Piers.

'No Gary,' echoed Piers thoughtfully. 'Thanks, John.'

The girls threw their coats over the landing banister and came in. Piers' room was popular because he always kept it warm. John handed them each a glass of cider. 'No Gary today?'

Beth shrugged and thanked him as Darren slammed the front door and pounded upstairs for company and heat. He made straight for the radiator and John passed over his glass of orange juice. Darren disapproved of alcohol. 'Here's to your poor poisoned livers,' he said, grinning. He looked at Beth over the edge of his glass. 'Didn't see no Gary today.'

Everybody felt her annoyance building. 'Why do you all go on about it? Maybe he's sick. How do I know? I'll go round and find out if that's what you want. He was okay when I saw him Wednesday.'

Her irritation brought silence to the room.

'Who's on lunch duty downstairs?' Piers asked. Morning worship at The Hut had been warm and loving. He didn't want the mood spoiled. There was a general groan from the entire room. He smiled. 'Any volunteers?'

Everybody looked down or away or whistled absent-mindedly. This was obviously a well-liked and practised routine.

'Come on,' said Piers. '*Somebody's* got to go.'

'I don't mind going,' volunteered John. 'I like Mrs T.'

'We all like Mrs T,' murmured Darren. 'It's just her cooking that's crap, man!'

There was some laughter. Piers didn't join in. 'They offer with a good heart,' he said quietly. 'Who'll go with John?'

He looked at Claire who emphatically shook her

head. 'I went two weeks ago,' she protested. 'It's Beth's turn.'

Beth was not in the mood. 'Is it hell!' she snapped.

'Yes. I think it probably *is* hell,' said Piers smoothly. 'Unfortunately somebody has to go down there with John and be company for the Turners over meat, gravy and two veg.'

'Me,' called Frankie, bursting in. 'Sorry I'm late.' She grabbed the remaining glass of cider from the table. 'Hey,' she called to Beth, 'where was your Gary then?'

Beth looked out of the window in dangerous silence but at that moment Mrs Turner's lunch gong sounded down in the hall. Everybody pointed and grinned at John and Frankie who bravely drained glasses, linked arms and set off for downstairs. The rest waited impatiently for the heartfelt – and very loud – greetings from Mr and Mrs Turner to their Sunday guests which never varied. 'Come in and God bless. Make yourselves at home.'

'We hope you've brought your appetites with you!'

Among the not-quite-silent applause upstairs, Claire produced a pen and notepad. 'Orders for Chinese takeaway please.'

SIX

At The Lion Gary sat in his room going over the long list of lighting changes for *The Merchant of Venice*. He really wanted to get this right. It mattered. The group was working well and Gary was accepted as an important member of the team.

He remembered his surprise and pride when the girl who was playing Portia had leaned over him for a look at his lighting chart, her hands on his shoulders. 'Done all this before, have you?' she asked, smiling and impressed. Gary had shrugged modestly.

There was a knock at his door and Eileen looked in. 'Somebody to see you downstairs. Lounge bar.' Gary quickly checked his hair guiltily. He had not seen Beth for two days and knew he should have been in touch but it had seemed easier to let it slide. Now here she was. He tested his breath and hurried down. The small lounge bar was almost empty. Derek and Eileen were talking to Harry at the counter as Gary pushed open the door.

'Eyup,' the old man said. 'Here's trouble.'

Eileen laughed and Derek moved into the public bar to serve somebody who was calling. Gary looked round for Beth.

'You might know my grandson,' said Harry proudly.

The figure at his side turned to face Gary. It was Kent Bailey.

Kent Bailey prowled round Gary's room scrutinising his possessions. Gary sat on the edge of his bed, head down. He couldn't believe this, didn't know how he had managed to survive the last five minutes.

Kent Bailey picked up a robot from the bookshelf. It was a favourite toy – a Christmas present several years ago – but Gary saw it through other eyes now. It was cheap, childish, ridiculous. Kent Bailey tossed the figure back on the shelf and looked at the wall of posters. Gary felt ashamed of them too. At last the boy with grey eyes turned to address Gary. 'What you been telling him?'

Gary shook his head, not trusting himself to speak. He was in his own room in his own house but thought he might begin shaking any moment.

'I'm talking to you.' Kent Bailey was also aware he was in Gary's home but although the voice was low it was menacing. And angry.

Gary forced himself to frame a hesitant answer. 'Nothing . . . just . . . the pool.'

'No names. You didn't give names?'

Gary shook his head. He fixed his eyes firmly on the floor. If he looked up he thought he would go to pieces.

'Who else you been talking to?'

'Nobody.' Gary's voice was a whisper.

Kent Bailey opened the wardrobe door. He scanned Gary's clothes indifferently and kicked it shut. 'He says you're having hassle from a couple of yobs. That's what he says. He says you went to his poxy caravan.' He was in front of Gary now. 'Look at me!'

Gary raised his head. He felt his lip shake.

'Keep away from him. You listening? One more word and we'll sort you out properly, Eddie and me.'

Gary felt his shoulders start shaking. He was scared what might happen and fought for self-control.

'You listening?'

Gary nodded.

'He's just an old man. Half mental. He must be to come to this dump every day. So keep out of his way. If my father gets to hear anything about this . . .'

He let the threat hang in the air. The shaking grew

worse and Gary dropped his glance down to the floor. Kent Bailey hissed through his teeth, a soft scornful sound. 'You and me – we're going down now, right? You say we had a good talk, right? And you're going to be okay up at the college from now on, right?'

Gary nodded. Kent Bailey clipped the back of his head aggressively. 'Stand up. Look at me.'

Gary slowly got to his feet. He felt the full power of the steely grey eyes. 'Next week, right? Next week I don't want to see you. We're going to look out for you – Me and Eddie – and if we see you up the colleges you're in big trouble. I know where you live now. Remember that. So stay away from the old man's caravan and stay away from your poxy Sixth Form College. This is a test I'm giving you. You better pass it. Right?'

He walked from the room and Gary followed. Downstairs, in the lounge bar, Derek gave them each a shandy and Harry told them gardening stories. Gary did his best to be cheerful. He was too frightened to be anything else.

'Nice of Harry to bring his grandson over to see you,' said Eileen.

They were having a cup of tea together while Derek was getting rid of the last customers.

'How did you get on?'

'Fine,' Gary murmured.

He felt she was probing, felt she must have noticed something. She laid a cool hand across his brow. 'Don't get overdoing things, my son. You get too involved. I know you.'

He took a mug of tea into the bar for his father who was swallowing a very large secret Scotch. The customers had gone.

'Good lad, that Kent,' he said. 'That's the sort of mate I want you to have. It's what you need. Somebody with guts. Not religious maniacs. Sportsman too, he tells me – he plays striker for the Tech. Sort of kid I like.'

Gary knelt in the dark of his room and urgently talked in his head to God. 'I don't know what to do. Help me, please. I know what you say about my enemies but I don't understand what you mean. I can't love my enemies. Why are they doing this? I've got to be there for the play, can't let everybody down. Don't let me freeze. Help me. Please. Make me strong. Show me what to do.'

For the first time since Gary had begun praying three years ago he felt he couldn't get through or that nobody was listening at the other end. His muddled emotions hijacked his prayers. He was in despair. Between Gary and his God, Eddie Watts and Kent Bailey were building a wall of panic.

He fell back quickly on familiar and trusted words. 'Our Father – may Your name be hallowed on earth as it is in heaven. Give us this day our daily bread and forgive our sins as we forgive those who . . . those who . . . who . . . Kent Bailey and Eddie Watts, Eddie Watts and Kent Bailey . . . sin against us and . . . and Eddie Watts and Kent Bailey looking out for me. Eddie Watts and Kent Bailey . . .'

The panic wall rose steadily brick by brick.

'Help me, please. *Please. PLEASE* . . .'

His heart pounded in his chest and the shivering was about to begin. He was making himself very scared. Gary rose very carefully from his knees and climbed into bed. He lay in the dark and fought a long lonely battle against his fears until he fell into a shallow, dream-ridden sleep which brought Eileen to his bedside at two-fifteen. After that he was more peaceful.

Next morning, apprehensive but determined not to let Mrs Bentley and the drama group down, Gary left the bus one stop earlier than usual. He had tried to pray in his bedroom and during the bus journey but with the same negative result. He hoped God was watching even though he didn't seem to be listening.

He took a different route to college. At the top of College Hill Gary slipped between a shop and a café to take an overgrown path which eventually led to the back of the Art College. After a couple of hundred metres it touched the oldest part of the whole college campus where a long-disused secondary school stood adjoining playing fields, locked up and ready for demolition. Most of its windows were smashed and Gary noticed rusty bike racks at the side of the building. Perhaps this would be a place to leave his machine.

He turned from the path into the Art College grounds and immediately began to meet students hurrying to their colleges. Gary had timed his arrival well. As he entered the Sixth Form College locker room he realised he was holding his breath and let it out in a deep sigh of relief. He swung round to shut the door and that was the moment he saw them – Kent, Eddie and Tina – deep in conversation, making for the Technical College. His heart jumped and – as usual – he froze as he watched intently. Gary couldn't tell if they had seen him. He thought they hadn't. He hoped they hadn't. He prayed they hadn't.

The dress rehearsal was nervous and unsure. Mrs Bentley's style of direction used as few costumes and props as possible – a hat, a pair of gloves, a scarf. Because rehearsal time had been short, her chief actors were allowed to carry scripts but it was a point of honour that they should have learned the major speeches. There was no scenery just an arrangement of rostra. It was left to Gary's lighting to create dramatic effects.

He began well, concentrating hard on the opening scenes, altering the shape of the acting space by carefully planned shadows and darkened areas, handling the changes smoothly on the lighting board. It was during long scenes when he had nothing to do that his thoughts wandered and created gaps in his attention through which his imagination showed the grey eyes of Kent Bailey an hour ago with Eddie Watts at his side . . . Eddie Watts Kent Bailey Eddie Watts Kent –

'Gary!'

His mind jolted back to the drama room. He had fallen two cues behind and the actors were waiting for the crucial lighting change. He fumbled to correct the error but his confidence was shaken and other mistakes followed. As the neon striplights flickered on at the end, Mrs Bentley came over to him and smiled sympathetically. 'You're allowed an attack of nerves just like the others,' she said. 'Let's hope you've used up your allowance.'

John was waiting outside the drama room. 'How did it go?'

Gary pulled a face and shrugged. They made their way along the noisy corridors towards the canteen. John grinned. 'It'll be all right on the night.'

'It'd better be!'

They turned into the canteen area. The noise, the stuffiness and smell suddenly hit Gary's nerves and stomach. 'Look, John, sorry. I'm not hungry. I want to go through the lighting cues again anyway.'

John understood. He smiled and lightly punched Gary's shoulder. 'See you then. Good luck.' John pressed on towards the canteen and was soon lost in the crowd. Gary turned and was pressing through the flow of hungry students when his arm was gripped and twisted, pushing him flat against the wall.

'I warned you.'

Gary stared wildly at Kent Bailey.

'I told you to keep out of my sight.'

Gary forced himself to stay calm. Nothing could happen here. There were students all round them. The pressure on his arm loosened as he looked into the cold grey eyes. Gary licked his lips nervously and controlled his breathing. He couldn't trust himself to speak. He shook his head.

'You what?'

The grey eyes suddenly gleamed. Gary looked sharply away. They had become animal eyes, incapable of reason and frightening. He took an instinctive step away but his arm was clutched again and he swung back against the wall.

'Look at me when I'm talking to you.'

Gary raised his head. The gleam had left Kent Bailey's eyes. They were cold and steely again.

'Get out of here. Now. This is your last chance – you better take it. If you're still here this afternoon, you're dead. Right?'

He jabbed a knuckle hard into Gary's chest three times – one stab for each word. 'You. Are. Dead.'

Tina stared disbelievingly at her boyfriend. She put down her Coke. 'What's *wrong* with you?'

'I'm standing by my mate. That's all.'

Tina looked at Eddie Watts, angry and frustrated. He glanced round the café, pleased there were few customers to hear the discussion.

'Me,' Tina said. '*I'm* your "mate". Not Kent Bailey. Right?'

'You know what I mean.'

'No, I don't know what you mean.'

Eddie hated bickering with Tina. He wasn't used to having his opinions challenged and was aware that she was more intelligent than he was. 'Just leave it out,' he growled. 'He's my friend. You've got to stand up for your friends.'

Tina couldn't believe what she was hearing. 'Stand up for him? Who against? What danger's he in?'

Eddie drank the last of his coffee and stood, picking up the sportsbag at his feet. Tina followed him silently to the till where he paid for their coffee and Coke. 'Listen, Eddie,' she said quietly as they waited for his change, 'Kent's getting big thrills from scaring this kid at the Sixth Form. That seems normal to you, does it?'

Eddie took his change in silence and made for the door. Tina spoke obstinately at his elbow. 'It's little boys' stuff. You don't need it.'

The rain had blown over but the wind was strong at the top of College Hill. Eddie and Tina walked towards the colleges for the last session of the day.

'Kent's my friend.' That was all there was to say as far as Eddie was concerned and Tina knew it. At the entrance to the catering block they turned to face each other and Eddie kissed her. 'See you tonight.'

Tina made a final attempt. 'Kent's a bloody nutcase if you ask me,' she said. 'And you're no better if you go along with his little games.'

'Tonight. About seven-thirty.'

He turned and walked into the building. Tina watched him out of sight before walking thoughtfully towards the computer rooms. She remembered what her mother said about men. 'They never grow up. They get stuck at ten years old. It's their big problem.'

'Why do women put up with it, Mum?'

'God knows. That's *our* big problem.'

Gary hadn't gone home. He sat alone at the lighting table waiting for the stage manager's signal. The drama room was stuffy with overcrowding. Second- and third-year drama students sat in the back rows or stood around the walls eager to denounce the production as inferior to their own first-year efforts. The GCSE students from the English department sat at the front with their lecturer Mrs Farrier, pleased at the novelty and keen to see the drama group make idiots of themselves and glad to have a lecture-free afternoon. A tape of Elizabethan dance music jangled above their chatter. How could anybody dance to that, thought Gary? It sounded dreadful. Still no signal. He watched Mrs Bentley talking to Mrs Farrier and looked through the first two pages of lighting cues. He glanced at the controls on his lighting board. He picked up the script, bent it flat again and turned to the first scene. At last the sharp beam of the stage manager's torch flashed on to the ceiling and flickered on and off. Gary began to dim the room's general lighting. He heard the audience settle. Gary concentrated on his work. If he relaxed he knew he would see grey eyes that gleamed and the first bricks would be laid in the wall.

Meanwhile Kent had spent the lunch hour shopping.

'I've got everything.' Eddie noticed an edge of excitement in his voice. Tina was right about Kent's thrills. He grunted noncommittally as he found the key to his locker. Kent looked at him anxiously. 'You're in with me on this, aren't you? He's asking for it.'

Eddie pulled out his white linen jacket. They would be making pastry this final session. He liked making pastry. 'I'm with you,' he murmured.

Kent took a neat plastic case from his locker and brought it across to Eddie. 'What d'you think?' He opened the lid. Eddie examined the contents with interest and Kent grinned, pleased. 'He's going to get a lesson he won't forget,' he said. He replaced the small case as the bell above the door announced the last session. They slammed their locker doors shut and made their way towards the kitchens. Kent spoke casually.

'You see Tina this afternoon?'

'Yeah.'

'She okay?'

'You know women.'

'Right.'

So, Kent thought, Tina and Eddie had quarrelled. What he'd got lined up for the Byrne kid would cheer his mate up. Women wouldn't understand.

The girl playing Gratiano smiled at his lover, Nerissa, below a single string of fairy-lights.

' "But were the day come, I should wish it dark
That I were couching with the doctor's clerk." '

They moved together in Gary's silver-blue moonlight and gazed at each other in a suitably smitten way. The horrible Elizabethan dance began as Gratiano triumphantly delivered the last two lines.

' "Well, while I live I'll fear no other thing
So sore as keeping safe Nerissa's ring!" '

All the drama girls who were acting men bowed to their partners who curtseyed back. Then everyone reverently kissed their scripts, tossed them carelessly over their shoulders, the trademark of Mrs Bentley's productions, and formed a conga line which snaked from the acting area, round the edge of the room and out through a side door as Gary smoothly and slowly brought the lights down to nothing, leaving only the string of coloured lights overhead. As the last chord of the dance died away he switched them off.

Cheers. Applause. Gary lit the stage brightly as the smiling actors re-entered to take a curtain-call and Gary felt the tension of the last fifty minutes begin to drain away. It was over. A near-perfect job from all concerned. The actors were pointing at him now and he found himself on his feet grinning stupidly and making a clumsy bow. Mrs Bentley winked at him and gave him a thumbs-up sign. A wave of strong feeling engulfed Gary. He was part of a good team, an acknowledged expert. It was a new feeling for him. He wished Beth could see him, wished his parents could see him, wished Piers could see him. Gary felt wonderful. He wished everyone could see him.

Kent Bailey and Eddie Watts looked down at the sixth-form students leaving. They were watching from a small lecture room at the top of the catering department. Kent was tense with expectation – like a hawk staking out a rabbit warren. 'What if we miss him?' asked Eddie.

'We won't.'

'He's taken your warning and pissed off home.'

'He's in there somewhere.'

Eddie began to catch some of his mate's excitement. This could be a good laugh. He was impressed by Kent. Like Tina said, he was a nutcase but you had to admire him. Kent was really into this.

NINE

At half-past four the cheerful college caretaker arrived to lock the drama room. 'Come on, son. Haven't you got a home to go to?'

Gary rose silently, picked up his bag and made for the door. The caretaker laughed. 'Cheer up! It's not as bad as that, is it!'

Gary was making for the library when the librarian passed him, jangling the library keys as he hurried out to his car. Gary was running out of places to go.

He was apprehensive to find the locker room empty. He had hoped to find someone he knew – anybody to leave the college with. Tiredness weighed him down. The tension of the performance had been replaced by anxiety about Kent Bailey and Eddie Watts. He slowly swapped books between bag and locker. His logic said it was not likely they were still out there looking for him but his fears told another story. He tried to pray but the wall immediately began to build. Kent Bailey Eddie Watts, Eddie Watts Kent Bailey. He had no sense of being heard as the ideas echoed in his mind and the panic wall rose higher.

'Come on, come on. You still here? You're not thieving, are you?' The cheerful caretaker was losing his sense of humour. Gary shut his locker and made for the door which the man was holding pointedly open. Gary had a sudden thought. He wondered if God had been listening after all and if this could be some strange answer to his prayers. He put his trust in God and walked out. The door slammed shut and was locked behind him.

Words were circling in Kent Bailey's head too. 'Come out. I know you're in there. You know I know it.

Come out and come out now.' He glared down and his eyes caught fire. He smiled slowly. 'Yes,' he whispered. 'Yes.'

Eddie Watts heard and opened his eyes. He lifted his head from the pillow of his sportsbag, twisted to his feet and came to Kent's side to watch Gary walk briskly towards the back of the Art College.

'Perfect,' breathed Kent Bailey.

Out in the stiff breeze, away from the campus, Gary felt more in control and quickened his steps. Two hundred metres past the disused school lay the safety of College Hill and the bus home. A tune from The Hut came banging into his head. 'A new commandment I give unto you . . .' He adjusted his pace to the rhythm and began to whistle. He was coming up to the school now. He could see where the drive bent round towards College Hill. But the wall was suddenly back.

'That ye love one another as I have loved you. Kent Bailey Eddie Watts Kent Bailey Eddie Watts. That ye love one another as Kent Bailey Eddie Watts . . .' His footsteps slowed in time to the beat of the names. Kent Bailey Eddie Watts Kent Bailey Eddie Watts. The rhythm was controlling his pace. He was walking slower. Kent Bailey . . . Eddie Watts . . . Kent Bailey . . . Eddie Watts. And slower. Kent . . . Bailey. Eddie . . . Watts. Kent. Eddie.

Gary stopped. The wall was complete and he could not cross it. He was calm – beyond panic. Gary looked up with no surprise to see Kent Bailey and Eddie Watts side by side before him.

Beth suddenly felt very cold and found herself thinking of Gary.

'Something the matter, dear?' Mrs Turner was looking at her. Beth unfroze, embarrassed at being noticed. She smiled. 'Nothing, Mrs T. Just felt a bit strange.'

'You're not sickening for anything, are you, dear?'

Beth shook her head. 'I'm fine.'

Beth finished dusting the Turners' sideboard. Maybe she would swallow her pride and drive to The Lion later.

Time seemed to stretch. Gary heard a soft low moaning rise from his throat. Kent Bailey took Gary's bag, polite as a hotel porter. Calm and reasonable, they each held an arm and walked him to a side door of the school. He seemed unable to resist and the low moaning continued.

Kent gently reassured his fears. 'Sssh, Gary. Come on. Ssssh.'

'Please. No.'

'Yes, Gary. Yes.'

Quietly they entered the dark unknown.

It had been some sort of basement cloakroom. Ranks of coat-pegs lined a wall above a jumble of broken classroom furniture and light filtered in through a cracked window curtained by sacking. It was an L-shaped room and round the corner four vandalised showers twisted from their fittings like small metal flowers on long spindly stalks. Eddie kicked open the door and they brought Gary down the six stone steps. The whole place smelled dank and musty. Sounds magnified as they bounced round the concrete walls. There was cigarette smoke. From a dark corner came whispers and a nervous laugh. Eddie shouted, 'Out!' Four boys of about twelve picked up briefcases and rucksacks and did their best to saunter carelessly across the room. Their uniforms showed they were pupils at the local high school whose playing fields adjoined the derelict building. They squeezed through the jammed door in turn and – once they were safely outside – jeered and catcalled back from the decaying corridor.

Kent hung Gary's bag on a peg and reached up to tug the sacking from the grimy window and intensify the late afternoon light. Gary was too numb for fear.

This was Kent's show but Eddie needed to stamp

his authority on the situation. He turned to Gary. 'You get lunch today?'

Gary could make no sense of the question. He tried to look the boy in the face and shook his head.

'Good.'

Eddie Watts punched Gary in the stomach folding him instantly to the floor. Choking for breath and totally involved with pain he rolled in the dust as Eddie watched dispassionately. Kent looked down at him with genuine interest as he emerged from the shock of the blow, still choking, still groaning.

Kent spoke. 'On your feet.'

Gary made the effort but was still hopelessly jack-knifed.

'On your feet, Gary.' Kent stepped forward to haul him to his feet. Gary stared desperately from face to face. Pain cramped his stomach again and he rocked forward. If he could have spoken, he would have begged for mercy.

'Let's go.'

They took him by the arms and shoved him towards a row of rusting metal lockers bolted to the wall. Gary felt he could almost talk. It was essential to tell them he had kept his word. He hadn't told their names to anybody and only Harry knew about –

He squealed in shock as they jumped him, slamming his back against an empty locker, trying to pack him inside. Gary hated confined spaces and struggled against them. Eddie saw the funny side of the manoeuvre. 'It's the anorak,' he giggled.

They unceremoniously hauled Gary back out and knocked away his hands as he tried to stop them jerking the anorak from his arms and shoulders. Everything was happening very fast. He saw the anorak beneath scuffling feet and then found himself hopelessly jammed in the locker. Seeing Kent Bailey pull a roll of white tape from his pocket he redoubled his efforts to lever himself out but Eddie leaned all his weight against him and grabbed his hair with one hand while the other slammed his jaws shut. The shock shook his whole skull. Dazed with pain he offered no resistance as Kent Bailey expertly taped his mouth shut and wound the last of the sticky tape round the back of Gary's neck.

Instinct stopped Gary fighting almost immediately. He was in a confined space, unable to inflate his lungs and now his mouth was blocked. He wanted to scream and shout but concentrated instead on breathing carefully through his nose. He had a cold and was still short of breath from Eddie's punch but he stopped thinking about what might happen next. Gary put all his will-power into using as little breath as possible and using it well.

There was a sudden crash. He felt one arm pinned to his side and the other painfully punched by metal. It took him a few seconds to realise they had slammed the locker door shut. He was more constricted than ever now but his shouting and pleading only produced confused noises and hurt his chest. He managed to force his aching arm to his side where it was less painful and stared wildly through the square four-inch grille that now framed his face. He saw Eddie pick up his trampled anorak and toss it on to the broken desks and chairs.

Kent moved forward. His eyes locked on Gary's through the mesh window. 'You've been asking for this,' he said softly, matter-of-fact.

There was silence. Gary could not break the glance. He felt like a rabbit transfixed in the glare of a stoat. He was petrified.

Eddie coughed. 'Where's the arrows?' he said, wanting to get on with it.

Kent pulled the small plastic case from his pocket and held it out. His eyes never left Gary's face. Eddie took the case and opened it.

'I throw first,' said Kent Bailey. He turned away, breaking his hold, and Gary's glance jumped to Eddie's hands as he took out three slim darts which he handed to Kent. The boy with the grey eyes drew a line in the dust with his toe and placed his feet precisely. He balanced the first dart in his fingers and leaned forward into his stance. 'This is for running to my dad's old man,' he murmured.

Gary had seen darts pitched a thousand times in the pub but never considered them dangerous. As Kent prepared to throw he wriggled frantically in his tight metal box and screamed behind his tape. He swung his head away as far as he could.

The first dart glanced off the mesh of the grille in front of Gary's face but the second was on its way almost immediately. Kent's aim was true again and the dart flashed through the air into Gary's terrified eyes. The back of his head slammed against the rear of the locker as he tried to jerk away from the trajectory. The dart's point penetrated the mesh but its shaft jammed in the grille before falling to the floor. The third missed the grille but its impact rang in Gary's ears. Eddie collected the darts and replaced Kent behind the pitching mark. 'You're trying to turn my girl against me.'

Gary swung his head wildly in denial but his protest was muffled. Eddie's darts flew very fast and hard.

BANGBANGBANG. They exploded and ricocheted around the wire two inches in front of Gary's terrified eyes. Eddie whooped loudly. He ran to the locker and followed up with a deafening open-palm slap against the mesh. He kicked and thumped the metal door for good measure. Gary twisted and turned helplessly in his coffin.

Kent stepped to the mark in silence and lined up his shot. Gary shut his eyes. Behind the tape he begged and groaned.

'Open your eyes.'

Gary opened them to catch the missile already in flight. He slammed them shut again and crashed back his head, hearing the dart catch and collide in the wire before bouncing away. There was a pause. Gary listened intently. Nothing was happening. Kent was anxious to see the full impact on Gary of each throw.

'Open your eyes, Gary.'

The reasonable voice forced him to obey and he saw everything – saw Kent balance the dart and squint as he drew sight on Gary's face, saw his fingers flick and the dart fly, saw its course in slow motion. As he tried to screw away from the point the sound seemed slow and magnified too. Roaring echoes beat in his ears. Gary was shivering now. He could not stand much more. He did not know what he would do when he broke down but thought that if this kept on he would die. He felt utterly alone. At this moment he mentally surrendered.

Kent watched Gary keenly from the pitching line and recognised the submission in his eyes. He smiled and his grey eyes gleamed. He had trained and humbled Gary Byrne. Gary Byrne was his creature.

Gary acknowledged defeat. To complete his humiliation he felt warmth spreading in the lower part of his body, then coldness as the urine slid down his legs. A small shaming pool wet the dust below the locker. Kent and Eddie watched. Eddie spat. 'You disgusting git.'

Kent nodded understandingly. 'That is really gross, Gary,' he said softly.

Kent Bailey slotted the final dart back into the case. There was no need of it. Moving forward, he handed the case to Eddie and unlocked the door to peel away the tape from Gary's mouth as gently as he could. Eddie gathered the other darts. Gary's eyes stayed tight shut. He could not move. The tape pinched and wrenched his skin.

'Not a word, Gary. Right?' Kent demanded.

Gary nodded as the last of the tape was drawn from his face. Kent dropped it on the floor and spoke softly. 'Look at me.'

Gary's eyes opened. He looked blankly at Kent.

'We can do this any time. Any time we want. Or we

can do other things – this was easy. Next time . . .' He did not need to finish and turned to the steps without another word. Eddie spat again in Gary's direction as he followed.

Gary never moved. He heard the door jolted open and their casual chat as they walked along the corridor outside. Every now and then there was a scuffling blow as one or other kicked rubble from his path. The echoes dimmed and at last stopped altogether.

Gary never moved. He spoke to God in his head. 'Is this how it is?' he asked. 'When nobody needs you, there you are – lapping up the praise and worship. But where are you when things get really bad? Is this how it was on the cross with Jesus? You just went away and let him get on with it?'

Gary didn't expect a response.

He slowly edged himself from the confines of the locker. His jeans were cold and wet as he collected his anorak. He was trying to rub away the dust and grime when he was aware of movement near the door and the flare of a lighter. The smokers had returned. Gary took no notice. He tugged the anorak on and lifted his bag from the pegs. He had no idea what the smokers had seen or heard and he didn't care.

One called to him. 'Gary! Why did they want you?'

Gary took no notice. For some reason it became vital for him to check his books so he unzipped the bag and sorted through the contents.

'Gary – you're weird.'

'Hey, Gary – what college you at?'

Gary zipped up the bag. As he walked towards the door the youngsters moved away and he wearily began to climb the steps. There was a laugh of shocked delight. 'He's pissed his pants!'

'Gary!'

'You're really weird.'

One of the boys moved forward. 'Gary?' he said quietly.

Gary turned. The boy came to the foot of the stairs. He held out his cigarette. 'Want a drag?'

Their eyes met in a moment of secret sympathy – one victim to another – but Gary shook his head and went out into the corridor. It was very dark now. Through the rows of smashed windows he could see the orange glow of distant street lights. He was very tired and must walk home. He was too ashamed to risk the bus.

TEN

Gary came home slowly. For the first time for many days there was nothing on his mind: he was burned out. The Saint Barnabas clock struck the half-hour above his head. He was late. What could he say? He could say . . . could say they . . . His mind drained with the effort as he slouched into the street. And stopped. No lights at The Lion. No light on the sign. No lights in the bar window. Nothing to light up the car park.

His first thoughts were that the clock must be wrong or that he had mistaken the time himself – it must be half-past five, not half-past six – but a glance at his watch confirmed Saint Barnabas. Gary stared along the street. Lights shone from the houses either side; there was no power failure. For The Lion to be closed half an hour after opening-time made no sense. It had never happened before. Gary forgot excuses and quickened his step.

Gary opened the back door and turned on the light. He passed through the empty kitchen. He opened the stockroom door and looked in – nothing. He hurried along the corridor and glanced in the bar where embers were dying in the grate. Gary ran upstairs. No one in the bathroom. He pushed open the door to his parents' room.

'Don't put the light on.'

Gary took his hand from the switch, puzzled and worried. 'The bar's not open.'

There was no response.

'Where's Dad?'

His mother's voice was calm, almost lifeless. 'Listen to me.'

'Mum –'

'I'm going to tell you something. Something I promised I'd never tell anyone.'

Gary didn't like the voice, didn't like the dark. 'Mum?' he said again.

'We didn't move here to give you a new start or because you were unhappy. We left the Birmingham pub because of your father. Because of his drinking problem. Because he beat up a customer once. Badly.'

Gary was suddenly tense. 'Not me?' he breathed. 'Not my fault?'

'Your father was lucky. He was drunk but so was the man and the police decided not to take it further. Bellings insisted we moved from the area. They gave him one last chance. Nothing to do with you, Gary.'

Gary might have felt relief. Instead he was flooded with resentment – all those debts he had repaid Derek and Eileen when he didn't owe them anything, so many grateful prayers for his understanding parents, all the promises to do better and not let them down again. His voice was harsh and accusing. 'You let me think it was my fault.'

His mother's voice broke emotionally. 'Would you have preferred the truth?'

'Yes,' Gary shouted. He turned and switched on the light.

Eileen sat near the window in her cleaning overalls. The right side of her face was swollen with livid bruising and her left eye was puffed up, almost shut. She was holding a wet flannel against her cheek. She looked abject and ashamed. Gary quickly turned the light back off. For a while there was no sound at all.

'Did he do this to you?'

Gary knew where Derek must be and was halfway down the cellar steps before he realised he had no idea what to do or say. In the dim light he saw his father slumped on a stool across the table he used for the cellar paperwork. The bottle of whisky was three-quarters empty. As Gary stood before him, one eye opened. His lips motioned but no words emerged. He coughed and tried again. The head lifted slightly from his forearms. 'Mother's boy,' he sneered indistinctly. 'Mummy's little boy.'

Gary's silent reproach irritated him. He looked Gary up and down. His gaze stuck briefly at Gary's stained jeans but he couldn't frame the right insult. Instead, he spat, 'Get out of here! Go to church! Go to your nutters!'

The head lifted higher and swayed. The two red eyes focused on Gary and were angry at what they saw. 'Go to hell!'

Derek swayed to his feet. He clasped the edge of the table for support toppling the whisky bottle which rolled from the table to shatter at the man's shuffling feet. He swung a clumsy fist in the direction of his son. He staggered a pace forward and did it again. 'What's your problem?' he shouted wildly.

Gary stared at his father in horror. He could hardly believe what was happening. Suddenly he felt shapes of words forming. Then his tongue was moving. A high voice, angry and scared, threw words from his mouth, fast and terrifying.

'*Ethula essatty – amencor donatis an affrac – ethula donat efframe colmadic elutha . . .*'

Gary saw amazement and fear sharpen Derek's sullen features. He felt fear himself. He tried to twist his tongue into familiar words but the unknown language flowed and flowed. It was not Gary speaking. He could not stop. '*Gramant acknor akura withstall mant . . .*' The flow was faster, the volume increased. '*Kapala kapala kapala – min pockell amal . . .*' The voice was shouting now. Gary tried desperately to choke the words back. '*Finam bell fint cassaman fint tomen finam bell . . .*'

Gary could hear feet on the cellar steps. He began to panic as the words roared out louder and faster.

'Kasta grib pan tap pan tap an looth mina con distalla mandap.'

He felt his shoulders turned and Eileen's arms surround him. She spoke quietly, comforting him, reassuring him. He felt her hot tender cheek against his face. He realised he was not talking any more. Whatever it was had stopped. Silence. Nobody moved. Gary unwound himself from his mother's embrace and stood back. He looked at them both. Their eyes were wide with distress.

'Excuse me,' Gary said politely as he made for the door.

The keen evening breeze and the distant hum of traffic began to lead him back into the real world. He sat on the bench in the yard, elbows on knees, head in hands, trying to make sense of what had happened but his jumbled feelings confused him. What had happened? Where had the words come from? He shivered as much with alarm as cold. Darren had spoken in tongues on the ridge above Llanthony but that had not been frightening – not really . . . or had it? Why? How? The whole of his day rose up to overwhelm him. He began to cry. He wished he could pray – could find anything solid to cling to.

'Help me,' he said aloud. 'Help me. Help me.'

A voice spoke near his shoulder. He somehow thought it was the voice of God but dared not believe it. 'It's all right, Gary. Don't be afraid.'

He turned his head cautiously towards the voice, unsure if anybody was there at all, but Piers was there and Beth was there and Darren and Claire were hurrying from the 2CV and the next moment they had him safe in their arms.

While the young crowded round Gary in the kitchen trying to raise his spirits, Eileen and the pastor talked quietly together in the living-room. She was hurt and upset and didn't want strangers involved. Nevertheless she admired the way he was handling the situation and assured him that there would be no problem about Gary staying a few nights at 180 Victoria Road. She heard rapid steps in the corridor as Derek pretended nothing unusual had happened and rushed round getting the pub ready for a growing number of impatient customers waiting outside.

'We'll take good care of him, Mrs Byrne. We know Gary well. We all like him.'

Eileen nodded, too dispirited to discuss the matter much. Her face throbbed and she felt ashamed as if it were her own fault. Piers smiled, understanding, and pushed back his chair to stand. 'I'll go and talk to Mr Byrne now.'

She laid an urgent hand on his arm. 'Not now. I'll talk to him later.'

Piers sat again. He explained the legal position. Gary was too young to leave home officially. Even when he was sixteen he would need the permission of both parents.

'I give you permission,' Eileen said firmly. 'In any case, we're only talking about a few days – just until I sort matters out with my husband. Nothing permanent.'

Piers nodded and stood. 'And what about you, Mrs Byrne?' he asked. 'What about that face? Who's going to take care of *you*?'

Eileen could not meet his kind gaze. 'My husband's a good man,' she said. 'It wasn't him that . . . did this. It was the drink. It won't happen again.'

Piers hoped he could believe her. He leaned forward to touch her bruised face gently and murmured a brief prayer. Eileen could not easily bear such kindness from someone she didn't even know. She felt she might cry and abruptly called Gary to come up to his room and pack a few things in his bag.

'Are you sure about this, Mum?' Gary asked as he opened his sportsbag on his bed.

'Of course I am. You just go, son. It's better for you to be with your friends just now. It's only for a few days.

Your dad and I have got to sort things out.'

'I don't want to see him, Mum. Not yet.'

'He'll understand why not.'

Gary opened his wardrobe and checked the shelves. 'He could hit you again.'

'He won't.'

Gary nodded and went to the bathroom to collect his towel and toothbrush. Part of him thought he should stay and be part of sorting things out – no matter how unpleasant it might get. But most of him was heavy with the weight of the worst day of his life. He was in no condition to make decisions. Everybody seemed to know what was best for him and he was content with that. He would have liked to talk to God but that line seemed to be permanently down.

PART THREE

The ARK

ONE

They all gathered in Piers' sitting-room to make Gary welcome and support him with their Christian love. As he came through the door they stood and cheered, wanting him to feel he had taken a decisive and correct step in coming to The Ark. Frankie gave him a strong hug and passed him on to Claire and Darren for more embraces while John and Piers came forward with strong handclasps. He sat on the settee which was big enough for most of them to enclose him and was soon munching toast and drinking tea to the background beat of one of Claire's CDs. Beth closed the door and sat as near Gary as she could. She could feel their special relationship melt into the general emotion and she worried about the haunted look never far from his face.

Piers gestured to Darren to turn the music off and leaned forward in his armchair. Everybody waited for him to speak. He kept his eyes fixed on Gary's face. 'We just want to welcome you, Gary. You know we're friends and want to do anything we can to help you. We hope you'll stay for as long as you need – even longer if you want.'

'Amen to that,' murmured Claire.

'Wonderful Jesus,' whispered Darren.

'So welcome. Look on us as another family.'

'Your family in God,' John said quietly.

There was a murmur of approval. Frankie sat on the carpet leaning against the settee. 'I want to say something,' she said, turning to look up at Gary. 'You don't know us. Not really. You've been here visiting Beth and seen us worshipping in The Hut. But you don't know anything about the sort of people we are.'

Gary thought it over. It was true. He looked across

at Beth. Frankie saw the glance. 'We all know about you and Beth but she's a bit like you. She's not committed to the work of the YPF. Not yet. She will be.'

'Amen to that,' said Claire and Darren together.

'Everyone here's got a story to tell – probably a story that's nothing to be proud of. We're all sinners and we've all suffered because of it. And we've been helped. That's why God led us here. It's why you're here too. God's put you here to be loved and helped. Just let it happen, Gary. It happened to me and I'm a new woman. Thank God.'

The strength of Frankie's words drew an instant response. There was a loud murmur of support.

'I witness to that.'

'Amen to that.'

'Wonderful Jesus.'

They all looked at Gary. The moment had come when he was expected to speak – to say something important. Beth was uneasy and hoped he would say nothing to make him look foolish. She knew how easy it was when things got as emotional as this. Too much love could be as upsetting as too much hate. She saw his eyes fill with tears and moved quickly to hold his hands. There was no sobbing. Large tears dropped slowly from his cheeks. Everybody whispered love and support.

'I think we should say a prayer,' said Piers quietly.

Gary spoke clearly. 'God's not interested.'

If Gary's distress and voice had not been so sincere they might have been shocked or argued with him. Instead a silence fell. It was Piers who eventually broke it. 'What happened today, Gary?'

The question was so gentle and casual that it was impossible not to answer. Gary's thoughts swayed around in the fog. He shook his head. He couldn't.

Beth squeezed his hands. Darren kissed his cheek. There were murmurs of support.

'Gary's tired,' said Beth. 'He should get some sleep.'

Nobody agreed.

'What happened today?' repeated Piers.

So Gary told them.

He told them how he woke up in his room at The Lion and what he ate for breakfast. It was not what they expected but it was the only way Gary could do it. He was following a trail through the fog and the further he followed it the less foggy his mind seemed to be. His voice strengthened as he spoke of the drama rehearsal and the panic wall outside the old school. It was hard for him to be honest about the locker room but the trail of events led him forward and by the time he was talking of his mother's bruised face the fog had disappeared. He was fluent. He didn't even stop at the point when Piers and Beth were suddenly at his side in the yard but went on to detail his arrival at The Ark. It was as if the whole tape of the day must be played or none at all. Gary concluded, 'And then Piers asked me what happened today.'

Nobody spoke for a long time. Darren let out a long sigh and reached for his guitar. 'So what we going to do?' he asked, strumming quietly. John looked across the room at him. 'About what exactly, Darren?'

Darren was suddenly aggressive. He crashed a harsh chord. 'Exactly about these bullyboy dudes, man,' he said.

Frankie agreed. That part of Gary's story had angered her too.

'Gary says he couldn't find the Christian way of dealing with it,' said Piers. 'Anybody here help him with that?'

'Not by turning the other cheek,' said Claire. 'Gary's right about that – he'd only get hit again.'

'Love your enemies?'

They looked at John who shrugged. 'I know it's hard,' he added.

'It's impossible,' muttered Beth.

Piers disagreed. 'Depends how it's done. Tell us more about this bullying, Gary.'

Gary related the incident at the Vincent Street Baths. Piers smiled.

'It's funny?' asked Beth, annoyed.

'In a way,' the man replied. 'I think I can see a way in which Gary can turn the other cheek, love his enemies and put down the mighty from their seat. With God's help of course.'

He looked enquiringly at Gary. 'And if he's got the courage.'

Darren had listened intently to the pastor. He began a stomping intro to a tune that was more of a march than a hymn. He sang.

'Our God is a God of War
And He is highly exalted.
Our God is a God of strength and song.
The Lord is a mighty warrior . . .'

Gary had never heard the tune or words before but it was well known to everybody else. Everyone except Beth joined in the chorus. Frankie and Claire clapped out the rhythm.

'We're singing and dancing and shouting and
marching
As we execute the justice and rule of our God.'

John stamped the floor. Piers beat the arm of his chair. The volume grew. Beth and Gary stared round them in wonder at the strength of purpose that was filling the room. Then Gary was clapping too. It was irresistible. Beth pulled his head down and kissed him hard. Their eyes were shining.

Downstairs, checking the windows before going to bed, Mrs Turner called her husband from the kitchen to listen. They stood side by side, beating time, his arm round her waist, singing a hymn they knew well. Someone was for it, Mr Turner thought cheerfully. It was the marching song of The Hut and made 'Onward Christian Soldiers' sound like 'All Things Bright and Beautiful'.

'We'll take the nations for Jesus
As Satan's kingdom falls.
Righteousness and truth will prevail –
Through our God!'

Mr Turner was right. Someone was for it.

TWO

The campus was busy at lunchtime. John called to Gary from the sixth-form library but Gary seemed not to hear him. John shouted louder. This time he turned. 'Can't come to Vincent Street this afternoon, Gary. Okay?'

Gary looked quickly round to see who else might have heard John's message. He raised a hand in acknowledgement and hurried towards the drama rooms. John turned back into the library and Kent Bailey looked across at Eddie Watts. 'Fancy a swim?'

From a window in the drama corridor Gary saw them walk up the steps into the catering block. It was the fourth day running that he and John had carried out this charade. This time it looked as if it might have worked. He hoped Piers knew what he was doing and turned to the phone at his side.

When he got to the pool it was its usual Thursday self. A few divers were carefully practising while a small crowd of swimmers thrashed happily in the main pool. There was – as always – a number of bathers shivering and chatting on the side.

Gary was quickly in the water trying hard to accomplish his underwater width. A record six strokes took him three-quarters of the way across but then he surfaced and turned to float on his back. He had never expected to be able to brave the pool again.

Tina looked down from the balcony and groaned when she saw Gary. She watched Eddie and Kent creep stealthily through the footbath and groaned again. So this was why they'd wanted to come. She had already annoyed Eddie by refusing to swim today and was prepared to let him know what she thought of him if they tried anything stupid. She was relieved to see an attendant on duty.

Kent Bailey and Eddie Watts drew back as Gary let his feet drop and looked round. He was getting cold but decided on another underwater attempt. He let go of the rail, put his hands before him, dropped below the surface and kicked away from the side. Kent Bailey and Eddie Watts immediately slipped into the pool at the deep end. Like sinister submarines they slid through the water to Gary.

Darren had been keeping watch while practising his springboard dives. He crossed the gap between the pools in four fast strides. John had been shivering with Claire and Frankie on the side. They were glad to jump in. The attendant looked idly round at the sudden entries but at that moment a tall well-dressed man appeared, carrying a camera and raised a friendly arm. As the attendant walked towards him, Frankie's elder brother Phil quietly slipped into the shallow end, with Beth, and Nathan – Darren's spectacularly muscular cousin – turned from cleaving the water with a strong well-practised crawl and made his way towards where the submarine warfare would begin.

Eddie Watts and Kent Bailey glided menacingly through the water, only to be met by the even greater menace of Darren, Cousin Nathan and Frankie – all strong swimmers – who swam very close alongside. As Kent and Eddie attempted to turn towards Gary they found themselves edged away. After two confused and unsuccessful attempts they shot angrily to the surface to find Gary in about a metre of water with several people barring the way.

Worse still, all these people were smiling at them. It was very unnerving. Cousin Nathan, Darren and Frankie surfaced and positioned themselves between Gary and his would-be assailants. They smiled too. Kent and Eddie noticed that Phil's smile was not a nice smile.

Up in the balcony Tina choked on her orange juice

but down at the side of the pool the attendant wasn't sure if anything was happening or not. 'Hey!' he shouted to the group in general.

All but two turned to him in polite enquiry.

'Watch it,' he finished lamely.

The well-dressed man spoke. 'I'm Pastor Latham from the Geldorf Avenue Ministry. That's some of my youngsters in there. Is it all right if I take a few pictures?'

The attendant's attention returned to the pool. Something was up but he didn't know what. He hadn't time to deal with this priest or pastor or whatever he was. 'Fine. That's fine,' he said, walking away.

'Everybody smile,' called Piers. There was a flash as he took the first photograph.

'What's your problem, man?' smiling Darren asked Eddie Watts.

'You what?'

'Man – your English is even worse than mine,' grinned Darren.

'*You what?*'

'You did it again, man.'

While Eddie Watts scowled and wondered what to do, Kent Bailey suddenly duck-dived and flicked through the water towards Gary. He hit four female legs and splashed to the surface flustered. Claire and Beth smiled at him. 'Why don't you go home to Mummy?' suggested Claire sweetly.

Kent was furious and thrashed water at them as the camera flashed. They both screamed very loudly. The bewildered attendant swung round. 'What's going on?'

Claire pointed to Kent, outraged. 'He wants to keep his hands to himself.'

'You,' shouted the attendant to Kent Bailey. 'Come away from there. If you can't behave, get out.'

He watched for the slightest sign of dissent. Frankie and Beth had their backs to the man. They both smiled sweetly at Kent. 'Pillock!' Beth whispered.

The attendant saw Kent Bailey's face change. 'I'm

warning you,' he called.

For a moment nothing happened, then Kent Bailey turned and swam angrily away. The camera recorded his defeat. As he glared up at the photographer Piers took another picture of his displeasure.

Eddie stood, hands on hips, glaring at Darren, John and Phil who now confronted him, smiling. Just behind them Cousin Nathan drifted easily in the water.

'How can anybody as stupid as you be so ugly with it?' Phil asked him in a spirit of idle enquiry.

'*YOU WHAT?*' he roared.

'Man,' smiled Darren reprovingly, 'ain't you got no conversation at all?'

Eddie snapped. He drove hard for Darren. 'Bloody coon!' he shouted.

Kent turned to attack with his friend but their opponents refused to play. Kent and Eddie began throwing punches and the camera shot some excellent action photographs. Piers missed the one where Darren kicked a sly backheel into Eddie Watt's stomach and Frankie kneed Kent Bailey between the legs – which was just as well since they had promised the pastor they would offer only passive resistance.

The attendant's whistle shrilled. All eyes were drawn to the main pool where two clear aggressors were trying to pick a fight with a number of innocent bystanders who were plainly appalled at the prospect. Tina shook her head, picked up her bag and made for the stairs as Eddie and Kent were ordered from the pool. For a moment they refused, turning viciously back upon the YPF and their friends.

'We'll get you,' shrieked Kent to Gary.

'Out.'

Kent and Eddie glanced uncertainly at each other.

'I said out.'

'He said out, man.' Darren was not smiling now. Nor were any of them. Frankie began a chant. 'Out – out – out – out –'

Eddie turned first and swam for the steps at the deep end as if it were no big deal. Kent followed less willingly. As they pulled themselves from the water Piers photographed their sullen exit and a cheer went up. Sensing trouble, the off-duty attendant came from the shower area to make sure Kent and Eddie left the poolside. Kent turned one last time and gestured obscenely to the world in general before the man hauled him through the footbath and towards the changing-rooms.

Suddenly it was all over. Darren and Cousin Nathan made for the diving pool with Phil. Frankie and Claire decided on a hot shower. Gary moved towards the steps but Beth called him back. 'Come on. Your underwater width. You can do it.'

Gary was only just beginning to realise the extent of his victory. Things had turned out well. Piers had told him they would. He was apprehensive about Kent Bailey's final threat. He smiled at Beth and shook his head.

'Yes. Come on,' called Frankie. She got back in the water. 'You can do it.'

Claire joined them. John swam over and Piers aimed his camera. Gary didn't manage the whole width but made nine strokes before he had to shoot up into the air snorting and gasping to general applause and the flash of the camera.

'Next time,' shouted John, grinning widely.

Gary nodded happily, breathing hard. 'With a bit of help from my friends.'

'Count on it,' said Beth, hugging him tight, kissing his lips.

'What a photograph!'

'Did you get that?' called Claire to Piers, laughing.

But Piers turned away to watch Darren and Nathan dive from the high boards.

Tina met Eddie Watts and Kent Bailey as they came

from the changing-rooms, angry and indignant. The off-duty attendant kept a casual eye on them. If they hoped for sympathy they were disappointed. 'Serves you bloody well right,' she said.

Eddie turned on her. 'Leave it out,' he muttered.

'No. I won't,' she replied.

'That Byrne kid is going to suffer some serious pain,' Kent Bailey said quietly.

Kent saw the afternoon's events as a personal insult. Tina watched the gleaming grey eyes disbelievingly.

'Right,' agreed Eddie Watts.

'Wrong,' said Tina. She stood in his way. He was forced to stop and take notice of her. 'Enough is enough,' she said. 'No more.'

Eddie was surprised and uneasy at her new forcefulness. 'You what?' he said without conviction.

Tina sighed. 'That black boy is right. You don't have any conversation.'

Eddie frowned and glanced at Kent, embarrassed to be confronted by a girl. Kent understood and looked tactfully away.

'You're going to be a father, Eddie. Which means you've got to start growing up fast.'

He gaped at her. His lips began to shape 'you what' but she got in first. 'I'm pregnant,' Tina said. 'That's why I didn't want to swim. We're going to have a baby. I've been waiting to tell you.'

Eddie began to smile. He began to grin. He began to cry. He grabbed Tina in an embrace. She was crying too. They had forgotten Kent who turned silently and made for the town centre. He was on his own now – one more reason to make Gary Byrne suffer.

THREE

Piers sat in the YPF van and watched his group walk along Tudor Close – Darren with his guitar, Frankie cradling her Yamaha keyboard and Claire warming up her flute. Beth and Gary walked with their arms round each other, as usual, and John followed a pace behind. Piers looked round to see who was about. Nobody. It was a quiet night – but not for long. Lucky that Harry had given Gary Kent Bailey's address.

Inside Number Sixteen the Bailey family were passing a typical night, except that Kent was home and making everybody edgy with his touchy mood.

'If you don't want to stay in, go out,' muttered his mother as she squeezed past him for the third time in the small kitchen. She put away the cutlery and tablecloth. 'Haven't you got any college work to do?'

Kent nudged open the fridge door and helped himself to a new carton of milk.

'Hey,' his mother protested. 'If you want milk there's a carton already open and that tall see-through thing on the draining-board is a glass.'

A young girl's voice called from another room. 'Mum – it's starting.'

Jean Bailey hurried to the kitchen door. She turned to Kent. 'And close the fridge door properly for once, please.'

Kent tapped it shut with his foot and gave her his blank look. She left. Kent thought it over yet again. Eddie and Tina engaged; he couldn't believe it. Eddie wanted him to be Best Man. No way. Kent felt badly let down. Eddie as a father was weirdest of all. He knew Eddie had been having fun with Tina. Kent had never thought it was serious. Kent stalked round the kitchen table drinking the milk. Eddie wouldn't finish the Catering Course now. Tina's father had a newspaper and tobacconist business in Station Road and he'd always wanted Eddie to join him in running it. And what about the Tech College team? That prat Davies would be captain now. He left the glass in the sink. He had a choice – play music alone in his room or join the rest of the family watching television. He could hear a lot of shouting through the living-room door. It must be *EastEnders*.

'Okay?' Darren looked enquiringly at Claire and Frankie. Frankie said yes and Claire gave a soft experimental blow to the flute and nodded. Darren grinned at Gary. 'Okay?'

Gary took a deep breath. John touched his shoulder. 'You're sure it's Number Sixteen?'

Beth smiled. 'It had better be.'

'Okay,' Gary said.

Darren turned back to his fellow musicians. 'One – two. One and two and . . .'

A sweet flowing tune began. Darren thought it was too slow and moved the pace a little faster. Beth tightened her arm round Gary's waist. The introduction came to an end and everyone watched Darren. He nodded. Everyone sang.

'Jesus, Jesus, Jesus – your love has melted my heart . . .'

Piers hummed the tune and tapped the rhythm on the steering-wheel. The hymn sounded very good in the silence of Tudor Close. His youngsters stood grouped on the pavement directly outside Number Sixteen's gate. Like John, Piers hoped it was the right house. A curtain moved across the road. Good. And another. A face appeared at Number Seventeen. Piers smiled happily and hummed louder.

In the Bailey living-room nobody at first connected

the street singing with themselves. Sally – Kent's young sister – shifted the curtains to look out.

'Sally! No!' said her mother. 'Go into the hall if you're that interested.'

Duncan Bailey reached for the remote control and increased the volume of *EastEnders*.

'Too late for carol singers, my boy,' laughed Harry to his sullen grandson.

Sally was already in the hall.

'Find out what they're collecting for,' Jean called to her daughter.

Sally Bailey opened the front door and stood shyly on the step. Six people were singing on the pavement. A couple of neighbours had come to their doors too and three of her friends came running along the road. Sally thought it was a bit strange that they were outside her gate and were singing directly at her house.

'Jesus, Jesus, Jesus – your love has melted my heart . . .'

She backed inside and shut the door.

'Jesus, Jesus, Jesus – your love has melted my heart . . .'

The repeated line rose over the quiet Close. Frankie tried a new embellishment on the keyboard and Darren grinned.

The front door of Number Sixteen opened again and Sally peeped round her father's legs. Harry stood at his son's side. He and Gary saw each other. Duncan was anxious to know what was happening outside his house but it didn't seem right to break into a hymn. He still thought they were collecting and wondered what bad luck had led them to his gate. Then the music stopped and Frankie prayed. 'Jesus Lord – look down on us here in Tudor Close as we help our brother Gary who suffers as a result of a fellow human. Lord – bless this house, Number Sixteen, and melt the heart of your child Kent Bailey so that he fulfils your commandment that we love one another.'

There was a startled silence. Sally giggled. 'She said Kent's name!'

Jean Bailey joined the cluster in the doorway. 'What's going on?'

Harry suddenly thought he knew and hoped with all his heart that he was wrong. He turned back into the house. He didn't want to see Gary just at the moment. Duncan shouted, 'Kent!'

Kent Bailey sprawled in the chair, pretending he had not heard and fixing his total attention on Albert Square. One quick look through the curtains had confirmed his worst fears. His grandfather came into the room. Their eyes met. 'Your dad wants you, Kent,' said Harry very quietly.

Kent never moved. Harry took a few paces towards him. 'And he wants you now!' The voice was suddenly hard. Kent heaved himself from the armchair and sauntered into the hall, trying not to show his fear. Maybe he could get away with it. Harry followed the boy from the room but turned to the kitchen for his coat and gloves. He walked out into the back yard and wheeled his bike towards the gate at the bottom of the garden. He could hear the voices at the front of the house and felt very old and sad.

'Wonderful Jesus,' called John. 'Wash Kent Bailey in your blood of repentance. Let him know in his heart the hurt he gives to our brother Gary.'

Duncan Bailey stepped forward. 'That's enough of that. What's this all about?' Duncan was aware of friends and neighbours.

Fifty metres down the road Piers' glance sharpened. This was the crucial moment. He opened the van door, ready to intervene if necessary. There was no need. John quietly and precisely outlined the problem. He was an experienced public preacher and speaker.

Duncan turned to his son. 'Is this true?'

Kent shrugged and kept his eyes on the path. It was enough of an answer.

'Inside,' Duncan said to Kent.

Turning back, he told John to wait on the pavement and ushered his family inside. The door closed firmly. Beth, Gary and the others looked anxiously at each other. Darren strummed a gentle chord and sang.

'A new commandment I give unto you – that you love one another . . .'

Nobody joined in and as his voice impressed the Tudor Close residents Beth laid her head on Gary's shoulder and Frankie draped arms around John.

Inside the Bailey house Jean pushed Sally towards the living-room. 'Watch *EastEnders* for me, love,' she said. 'So you can tell me what I've missed.'

Sally reluctantly moved to the lesser of the dramas and Jean shut the door behind her. Duncan lifted Kent's chin, forcing his son to look at him. 'Explain.'

'It wasn't only me.'

'Who else?'

'Eddie Watts.'

Jean stepped forward. 'Then you stay away from Eddie Watts from now on. How often have I told you?'

Kent protested. 'That Byrne kid – he *asks* for it, Dad. He does!'

'Don't be ridiculous,' said his mother.

Duncan's voice was reasonable. 'He asks for it, does he?'

Kent seized the slim chance of escape. 'He does. Honest.'

'Like *you're* asking for it now?'

'What?'

'And when he asks, you give it him?'

Kent was more guarded. He could not see where the conversation was heading. 'Yes . . .'

'Like this?' His father slammed his open hand hard against Kent's shoulder. The sheer force and surprise knocked him off-balance. He fell back against the coat-rack. 'And like this?' Duncan grabbed his arm roughly and swung him round so that he hit the opposite wall. 'And like this?' He swung Kent backwards against the foot of the stairs so that the boy sat heavily, confused and scared. He looked up fearfully.

'That's enough,' his mother said quietly. She stepped forward and drew Kent to his feet. She straightened his shirt where Duncan had tugged at it and smoothed back his hair. 'Now you're going out there,' she said, 'and you're going to tell that boy – going to tell them all – that it's over. Finished. The end. Right?'

The idea pierced Kent like ice. 'I can't,' he whispered.

'Yes you can,' his father said. 'Then you'll come back in and we'll talk it all over reasonably. You, your mother and me. We'll listen, Kent. We'll be reasonable. We promise. And then we'll close the chapter. But first get out there and make your peace.'

Jean Bailey opened the door. 'We're at your side, son.'

Through the open door Kent saw the waiting group, saw his neighbours. His father put a hand on his shoulder but he shook it off. He threw back his shoulders and walked out to make his peace.

'I bet the neighbours are loving this,' muttered Jean as she walked out with Duncan. A sudden thought struck her. 'Where's Dad?'

'In with Sally, I suppose.'

Darren's voice faded as Kent Bailey walked steadily towards Gary. There was a flash as Piers captured the handshake with the last shot in his camera. Then it was all over.

The adrenalin was still running high and the van journey home to The Ark was almost hysterical. They sang. They shouted. They narrated the anxieties they had felt. What if Kent Bailey had denied the charges? What if his father had called the police? What if Tudor Close had decided to unite against intruders? The day had been a triumph. The mood in the van was the same sort of feeling after particularly successful street preaching. They had been brave and had won. They stopped off for Chinese takeaways and cider. Piers paid for everything, wanting to reward his team. He had planned the strategy for both pool and Tudor Close but was as proud of the youngsters as if they had done it all alone. Everyone in the YPF van knew they had not done it alone, *could* not have done it alone. Wonderful Jesus had been there with them. Claire said she had felt him at her side every moment.

The celebration was so noisy that Mr and Mrs Turner looked up to the ceiling of their living-room with particular pleasure.

'We shan't get much sleep tonight,' Mrs Turner smiled.

'No,' her husband cheerfully agreed, turning up the radio.

A heavy thump set the central light swaying on its chord.

'Whoops-a-daisy!' laughed Mrs T, getting on with her knitting.

The thump had been Frankie and John falling from the settee locked together in battle for the last prawn cracker. Piers surveyed his room in great content. These were the times he loved best. Nevertheless he turned off the music and tapped an empty glass with a sticky knife for silence. 'All right, everyone. A great day, yes?'

There was a cheer of agreement.

'The best!' shouted Frankie.

Piers laughed and tapped again for silence. 'But it's way past eleven and most of us have to work tomorrow. So bless you all and good-night. We did the Lord's work today and no mistake. Now let's get this room cleared up – and no noise, please: don't forget Mr and Mrs T directly below.'

There was cheering and applause. Frankie, Claire and Darren crowded round Piers in a hug. Suddenly they were aware that Gary was on his feet in the middle of the room. They knew how uneasy Gary was about public speaking.

'I just want to testify here and now what Jesus has done for me today.'

There was an approving murmur and a few calls.

'Wonderful Jesus.'

'I witness to that.'

'Amen.'

'The Lord's shown me where my real family is,' Gary went on. 'And he's taken my troubles away. I don't have a worry in the world.'

Gary's voice began to break with emotion. Everyone understood. At one time or another, here or in The Hut, they had spoken such words before their friends.

'I don't know the words. Just wonderful Jesus – that's all I can say. Wonderful Jesus.' Gary suddenly shouted in total happiness. 'Wonderful Jesus! I'm full of love!'

They shouted it back to him, clapping, cheering.

Gary went to college the next morning with complete confidence. Now it simply did not matter if he met Kent Bailey or Eddie Watts. Things were different. He had true strength on his side: his friends and his faith. Kent and Eddie had become irrelevant. As if to prove the point they kept their distance and Gary's love for Beth and the YPF grew steadily.

The following Sunday The Hut had a visiting speaker, a pastor from another town, an old man who spoke with a soft and simple sincerity. Everyone waited for the important moment. Gary and Beth stood at the back, arms round each other, hardly breathing in the tense silence.

'The Lord gave his blood for you on Calvary Hill.'

The preacher's face softened to a sad smile as he pointed round the packed hall. 'And for you.'

He pointed again. 'And you.'

His finger travelled on. 'And you and you and you.'

Darren's musicians began playing very softly. The preacher took two steps forward. 'Open your hearts. Let in the love which the Lord created us for. Come forward with your fears and your doubts. Through the suffering of the Lord all this can change. Wonderful Jesus.'

There was a quiet echoing murmur from the listeners. 'Wonderful Jesus . . .'

The preacher slowly raised his arms. 'For all of us he gave his blood.'

John, Frankie and other members of the YPF gently eased back the people to create a path to the preacher. There was a buzz of expectancy and the tempo of the music increased still further. The preacher's face creased into genuine pleasure. 'Come forward,' he said softly. 'There are those here who know I am speaking especially to them. Step here to me. Be born again in the spirit.'

His voice rose. 'Die to your old self and rise with Jesus to be a new woman, a new man.'

Darren nodded to his musicians. The volume and tempo moved higher.

'This is his promise. Newness of heart. A new beginning. A new baptism in the spirit.'

Gary knew he must go forward. Already two others were making their way along the corridor in the centre of the room. Beth felt his tension at her side.

'What is it?' she whispered.

But Gary was unable to answer. What was happening made total sense to him. He was beginning a new life. He had passed through a time of doubt and suffering. Like Jesus, he had despaired because God had seemed to reject him. Now he saw the truth. Beth was uneasy. She mistrusted these shows of emotion and tightened her hold round Gary's waist but he turned to look at her and she saw his eyes were wet with tears. Seeing they were tears of love and knowing she must not prevent him, Beth withdrew her arm. He smiled and gently kissed her. Then Piers was at his side.

'Let it happen, Gary,' he said quietly. 'Open your heart. I'll be with you.'

And John was suddenly at his other side, recognising what was taking place and remembering his own decision to step forward and declare himself for God. A steady stream of people was moving down the centre of the hall. Gary needed Beth's approval. He turned to her and put out an arm.

'Come with me.'

But she was not ready and shook her head. Piers and John moved Gary away.

'Love is patient and kind,' the preacher was saying. 'Love isn't jealous or conceited or proud. It isn't ill-mannered or selfish or irritable. Love doesn't keep a list of grudges. Love isn't happy with evil. It's happy with the truth. Love never gives up, my friends, and believe me – believe Saint Paul – believe your Bible – love's faith and hope and patience never fail.'

Gary stood before the old pastor and felt a sense of wonder and rightness. He was firm in his faith. He was surrounded by his friends. He had found his place. He had found his woman. Love meant everything. It all made sense. He closed his eyes, overcome by the rightness of it all.

'Wonderful Jesus,' he whispered.

FIVE

Gary found his new life wonderfully different. As the preacher had promised, he felt he was another person or rather that some extra dimension had been added to what he used to be. His Christian life became one focus of this new world and his love for Beth the other. The other occupants of The Ark found the romance touching and amusing. Everybody understood Gary's new-found zest for life and whether it was due to God or to Beth was irrelevant – it was God who had brought them together in any case.

They had given him the room at the top of the house. It was very small – just enough room for a bed, a table and a curtained alcove for clothes. The only other room on the floor was John's. Piers' flat was on the floor below, with Frankie's and Beth's bedsits. Piers' living-room was the general meeting-place, even for Claire and Darren who didn't live there.

In his new life Gary did not forget about his parents and their problems but he had other priorities. His new life was at The Ark and The Hut with Beth and his family in God.

Gary and Beth spent most of their time talking and Gary talked most. It was wonderful to be with someone who seemed to find everything about him interesting. In return, Beth told Gary very little about herself.

'I don't know anything about you,' he complained as they sat crammed together in her armchair. 'I don't even know where you live.'

'I live here.'

'You know what I mean.'

'Ever been in Buckinghamshire?'

'No.'

'Well, that's where my family live. Satisfied? You want more? Right: I dropped out of college. I'm taking a year off. What difference does it make?'

Gary stroked her hair. 'Sorry. I didn't mean to . . . you know . . .'

There was an awkward silence then Beth suddenly turned and kissed him. 'No,' she said. 'It's me that's sorry. I don't know why I get so uptight. I come from a little village near a place called Brackley and the end of the story is that just before Christmas the 2CV broke down on the motorway and the garage I phoned towed it here.'

'What about The Hut?'

'I was waiting for them to finish the repair and I heard music – carols. It was the YPF out in the street. We got talking. I went back to The Hut for mince pies and I told Darren I needed somewhere to spend the night. He brought me here and introduced me to Piers. Next day the car was ready but I stayed on and don't ask me why because I don't know. You religious freaks will tell me God works in a mysterious way.'

Gary grinned. 'I thank Him for screwing up your rotten little car.' They kissed again. 'Do you know the worst thing that could have happened to me?' he asked. 'I might not have gone to that vigil, might never have met you – or the YPF.' He held her very close. 'I love you,' he murmured.

She drew away at once.

'What's the matter?' he said, surprised.

'You don't understand,' she said. 'Love puts everything on a high. Feelings get distorted.' She stood up and moved to the door. 'I'll make some tea.'

Gary went to her cupboard and found two mugs. He found Beth complicated and her attitudes towards the YPF made him uneasy. She was openly critical about some of their work and found their fundamental belief in the Bible absurd. To Beth the Bible was just a book – or a selection of books – and she couldn't see why every single word, translated and retranslated over thousands of years, with errors creeping in at every stage, should never be questioned.

She had no interest in finding a job either and earned her keep by cleaning and shopping for Mr and Mrs T who were fond of her. Piers always defended Beth by calling her the YPF's tame conscience. He claimed that although her part in God's plan was obscure, he would no doubt reveal it in his own good time. Gary had to be content with that. After all, it was what the pastor had once said about Gary himself.

Where Beth was cynical, Gary was desperate to demonstrate love and gratitude for his family-in-God. He prayed for the confidence to step forward like John, Frankie – even Claire – and regularly witness to God in public places. He longed for the courage to make difficult hospital or home visits like the others. In the meantime, he tagged along and did what he could in the background. But that wasn't simple either. With the inner circle of the YPF there *was* no background. Everything was upfront. Life with the YPF was all or nothing.

Gary left Beth's room to borrow a couple of tea bags from Frankie. It would all come right. He had perfect trust in the Lord.

After five days without a phone call from Gary, Eileen came to The Ark. Mrs Turner let her in and shouted upstairs for anyone who was listening. She smiled at Eileen who was feeling strange to be there.

'He's a lovely boy,' Mrs T affirmed. 'We all like Gary.'

John came clattering downstairs.

'They keep me young,' Mrs T laughed, leaving her.

Eileen introduced herself and John offered to show her up to her son's room. They set off up the first flight.

'Who actually owns the house?'

'Mr and Mrs Turner,' replied John, slowing for

Eileen to catch up. 'That was Mrs Turner who let you in.'

They creaked along the first landing.

'We call the house The Ark,' said John, making polite conversation.

'Flooding in the basement?' asked Eileen.

He laughed. 'No. A sort of lifeboat for people in trouble.'

John realised he was on tricky ground and shut up. They passed Piers' door. 'That's where the pastor lives.'

'Mr Noah himself!'

They went on. John remembered his long legs and waited again for Mrs Byrne to catch him up.

'Is there a Mrs Noah?'

John laughed. 'He says he's got enough problems as it is.'

Eileen toiled up the final flight of stairs to the top landing. John knocked at Gary's door. 'Gary? Your mother's here.'

As they waited he politely shook Mrs Byrne's hand. 'I'm John, by the way. The one who's at the college with Gary.'

Gary's door opened a little and Gary looked anxiously out. Eileen smiled reassuringly. 'Hello,' she said brightly.

Eileen hated the room. It was poky and dim – like a cheap hotel. Beth straightened up from smoothing the bed cover and smiled.

'This is Bethan,' said Gary.

'Yes, I know.'

Eileen smiled and took Beth's hand. 'We met when you came to The Lion.'

Gary's mother looked round his room, trying to show approval but Gary wasn't fooled. 'It needs a bit doing to it. You know – paint and things.'

Nobody said anything. Eileen held out a large plastic bag. 'Packed you a few things from home. Socks, pants, shirts. A clock; everybody needs a clock. And there's a few goodies to eat.'

Gary took the bag and thanked her. Another silence fell. Beth stepped forward. 'Tea or coffee, Mrs Byrne?'

'Thank you. Coffee would be nice.'

Beth left the room, closing the door behind her. Eileen sat on the bed. There wasn't anywhere else to sit. Gary slid down the wall opposite and sat looking up at her from the threadbare carpet.

'Does Beth live in The Ark too?'

'Yes. The floor below.'

They both felt wrong but didn't know how to put it right. They were strangers, offering politeness where there used to be day-to-day familiarity.

'How are you, Gary?'

'Great.'

'You haven't phoned.'

Gary shrugged. 'Sorry. You know. Busy.'

She looked round the poky room again. 'Who pays for you, Gary? The rent and your food?'

'People from The Hut. The Turners. Have you met them? They own the house.'

Eileen took out her purse and held out a twenty-pound note. 'You must pay your way.'

Gary hated taking it but knew it would be useful. 'Thanks, Mum.'

He got up to kiss her and sat at her side on the bed. He raised the difficult topic. 'How's Dad?'

'He's fine.'

'He hasn't . . . ?'

'No.'

The mood was changing. Important things could be said.

'When are you coming home?' Eileen asked quietly.

Gary could not look at her. He spoke softly, carefully. 'I've found my place, Mum.'

'We miss you. Both of us.'

'I miss you too,' said Gary.

His mother took his hand and half-turned to him.

'Why don't you come home for a meal? Any time you want. Or Sunday lunch. Bring Bethan. Bring anyone.'

There was a long silence. 'Can't do it, Mum. Not yet.'

Eileen sighed. 'Your dad?' she asked.

Gary nodded.

'Aren't Christians supposed to forgive and forget?'

'I'm working on it,' he replied.

Beth tapped on the door and waited before she came in. Gary took his hand from his mother's. The girl smilingly laid a tray on the table. 'Frankie's just come in,' she said. 'She's cutting a few sandwiches.'

'Quite a little family,' said Eileen and didn't know why she felt so sad saying the word.

Gary and Eileen walked downstairs together. Some of the awkwardness had gone. Eileen asked about Piers as they passed the door to his flat.

'He works at the garden centre in Evesham Road. He's usually home by now. You'd like him if you got to know him properly.'

Gary enquired about Harry, remembering the last time he had seen him.

'I was going to ask if *you'd* seen him? He hasn't been to The Lion for a week or more now – one more good customer we've managed to lose.'

At the door they said an awkward goodbye.

'Gary – if you need anything – if it goes wrong – you know where to find us.'

'It won't go wrong.'

Eileen kissed her son and looked steadily into his face. She saw confidence and a greater maturity. She hoped he was right. ''Bye, son.'

'Say hello to Dad for me.'

Gary watched his mother hurry down Victoria Road. The YPF van drew up outside and Piers got out. Gary walked across the pavement to meet him.

'Was that your mother?'

Gary nodded. Piers locked the van door.

'Everything all right at The Lion?' he asked lightly.

Gary nodded again. They walked to the house silently.

'Was my mother crying?' asked Gary suddenly.

Piers shut the door behind them. 'No,' he lied. 'Why should she be?'

SIX

Eileen's visit left Gary feeling guilty. He had deserted his parents to work out their problems, had simply moved on and let them get on with it. The lifetime of debts he owed them and the memories of so many good times weighed heavily on him. Most of all he felt terrible about Eileen. He had left her alone. She could be hurt.

On the other hand, Gary was sharply aware that he was beginning to do God's work and had been called to do it with the YPF. How could this be wrong? He was talking with God in his head when Beth came in. She saw he was upset and came to sit by him on the bed. She kissed him and stretched out at his side. She did not have to ask what was wrong.

'It's what I told you before. You've got to look after your own life and not let adults screw it up for you. Your mother's been to see you and you feel bad. This is what they do. They give you presents and say nice things and before you know it you're soggy with guilt because they've convinced you that you don't love them enough. Don't let them fool you!'

Gary thought it over. It made sense – of a sort – but it didn't help his mood. 'Suppose so,' he murmured.

Beth sat up. 'If you're going to stick in this bad mood I may as well go.'

She swung from the bed and turned to him at the door. 'Get a grip, Gary,' she said. 'This last fortnight you've been good fun – a different person. I thought that's what you wanted. Stick with it.'

She gave him a last sharp look. 'And Gary? Don't let me down.'

Later that evening Gary helped load the van for The Helping Hand Club. Once a week the doors of The Hut were thrown open to the town outcasts. Alcoholics came along with tramps and druggies turned up too if they needed food, clothes or advice. Christian social workers were in attendance as well as a solicitor. It was the sort of do-gooding that Derek and many of his one-time customers massively disapproved of but to The Young Peoples' Fellowship it was the big night of the week because they were able to carry out directly the orders of Jesus – and even Beth couldn't deny that.

Gary always spent the night in the tiny kitchen brewing endless pots of tea, cutting mountains of sandwiches and washing up continuously while the more confident members ministered in the hall.

'All aboard!' John slammed the back doors and jumped into the passenger seat alongside Piers. Beth and Gary were jammed among the provisions. The moment the vehicle drove away it was clear to Gary that Beth had mentioned his depression to the others.

'Had a bad time then, Gary?' said Piers.

Gary didn't reply. His hand was close to Beth's but she didn't take it.

'"A man's worst enemies will be the members of his own family".' quoted John. 'Matthew: Ten, thirty-four.'

'Ten, thirty-six but who's counting?' corrected Piers smoothly. 'But John has a point. Keep in mind the story of the Lord's family turning up to see him while he was busy preaching. He kept a cool perspective.'

'He sent them away,' put in Beth.

'He didn't,' Gary replied testily, feeling under attack. 'He just said that anybody who listens to his message is as much his family as his real mother, father, brothers and sisters.'

'One up to Gary's Bible reading,' smiled Piers.

John called back to Beth as she tried to keep a grasp on the boxes of bread as the van jolted to a stop. 'I thought you didn't believe in the literal truth of the Bible anyway.'

'Oh shut up,' she murmured.

'Luke: Two, forty-one's a better instance,' Piers said as he waited for traffic lights to change.

'Boy Jesus left behind at the temple?' asked Gary.

'He told his parents, who were understandably anxious and annoyed to have mislaid him, that he had more important things to do than be a good boy – namely the work of his father in heaven.'

The lights turned green and Piers banged the van into first gear and then second. 'So think about *now* – not tomorrow or yesterday. There's a bunch of the Lord's needy people waiting for us at The Hut. Let's think more about them and less about ourselves.'

'Amen!' John shouted. 'I witness to that!' And they all hung on as Piers swerved round the roundabout at the end of Geldorf Avenue.

Eileen walked from the living-room and into the lounge bar. Although it was seven-thirty, the lounge was empty. She slotted a cassette into the tape machine and quiet Muzak crept into the background. Derek came to join her from the public bar where there were four silent customers. 'Hardly worth opening,' he said.

Eileen adjusted the volume of the tape and turned to Derek. 'If there's anything you've got to do – VAT, cellarwork or stocking-up – I can look after both the bars. Maybe it'll get busier in an hour or two.'

Derek was grateful for the offer. 'Can I get you a drink?'

'Wouldn't mind a tomato juice.'

Derek poured the juice for his wife. 'How was Gary?' he asked carefully.

'He doesn't want to come home yet.'

'You should have ordered him back.'

Eileen turned away in impatience. 'And what good would that have done? Don't you ever learn? It's a comfortable house – though his room wasn't up to much. They were nice people. Mostly young. Caring. I envied him.'

Derek stared at her sadly. 'You envied him?'

'Oh yes.'

'Then there's nothing to be said.'

'That's right,' she replied, moving into the public bar to serve a customer. 'Yes, sir?' she smiled brightly. 'What can I get you?'

The man was standing at the counter where Harry should have been. As she poured the bottle of light ale into a gleaming glass she thought of the old man, hoping he was well and that warmer weather might see his return to his place at The Lion.

SEVEN

Eileen was not the only one to have been thinking of Harry. Gary talked it over, late that night, with Beth. They were in his room, weary but pleased with the work that had been done at The Hut.

'I'm going to take the morning off college tomorrow. Harry must be feeling really bad to stay away from The Lion all this time.'

They were stretched out side by side on the bed as usual. Beth raised herself on an elbow and looked down at him. 'Okay. I guess he's feeling bad – like you say. But he's not going to feel any better knowing you've bunked off college.'

She rolled over and dropped her feet to the floor. Gary reached out to stop her but she shook away his hand. 'You're giving up too much of your college work lately. Even when you're working you rush at it.'

'You heard what Piers said. There are more important things than being a good boy.'

'The Hut will carry on with or without you,' Beth said. 'Nobody's indispensable. Not even the wonderful Piers – though he likes to think he is.'

Gary frowned. He didn't like Beth speaking like that. Everybody knew how much The Hut owed to its pastor. 'That's not fair,' he murmured.

'Life's not fair,' she said at the half-open door. 'Go to see Harry after college and I'll come with you. Deal?'

Gary nodded and smiled. 'Deal,' he agreed.

'And don't sacrifice your course work. Remember – I gave up college so I know what I'm talking about. Think of yourself a bit more.'

Mrs Bentley looked out of the window. It was a sunny

day and students milled happily about in the open air below the drama room. She turned to Gary. 'You asked for an extension for your last essay too.'

'I'm sorry, Mrs Bentley.'

'What's taking up so much of your time all of a sudden? I spoke to Mr Swift and Miss Field this morning. They tell me it's the same with your English and economics.'

How could Gary explain that being a new man entailed other priorities? He looked down at his feet, hating this. He liked Mrs Bentley so much.

'You're not in any trouble at home?'

Gary shook his head. How could he explain? Mrs Bentley turned from watching the students. She smiled a little, puzzled and disappointed. 'Can you let me have the work after the weekend?'

Gary's brain raced through The Hut's timetable. Teenagers' Bible class tonight; adult discussion group tomorrow but he and Claire were on duty to provide the coffee and biscuits and clean up afterwards; youth club the night after. Sometime he had posters to put up in shop windows and Piers liked to take him home-visiting on Saturdays to pray with the sick and elderly. Then there was Sunday.

'No problem,' he said – wishing it were true and trusting in God to make it happen.

After college Beth and Gary walked hand in hand along the lane to the allotments on the edge of town. The spring weather had continued all day. Away from traffic the birdsong sounded deafening and the trees were definitely putting out new leaves. Gary and Beth grinned at each other in the sheer pleasure of being in the country – even if only by a couple of hundred metres.

Harry was digging in front of the caravan, involved in careful spadework. He didn't notice them until they were almost at his side. Gary smiled widely, pleased to see him and relieved to find him fit. 'Hello, Harry.

Thought I'd bring Beth to see you.'

Beth smiled and said, 'Hello.'

Harry continued his digging without a word or look. Gary and Beth glanced at each other. Gary tried to put him at ease. 'It's all right, Harry,' said Gary. 'Really it is.'

The old man raised a spadeful of loose soil and let it drift from the blade. He stuck his spade into the ground, straightened up with difficulty and turned to face them.

'All right, is it?' he asked bitterly. 'All right to make a fool out of my son and his family? All right not to tell me I was making a fool of myself when I brought young Kent to see you? I thought you and me were friends.'

Gary was horrified. 'Of course we're friends,' he said desperately.

Harry reached for his spade. 'That's not how friends behave in *my* book,' he said quietly.

He plunged the blade in the soil and continued his painstaking work. Gary and Beth stood foolishly at his side. They didn't know what to do.

'Gary says it's great inside your caravan,' said Beth. 'Can he show me? I'd really like that.'

'Would you?' said Harry, not looking up. 'Well, miss, we can't always have what we want. Good day.'

Gary stood, cold like stone. Beth drew him away with difficulty and they walked towards the town in silence, hearing only the senseless chatter of birds and the steady stab of Harry's spade growing quieter behind them. Beth knew how Gary must be feeling and kissed him. They came to the first road of the town and she held him very tight. He gave her a small smile and a brave shrug but he felt terrible and it was no surprise that the evening's Bible quiz at The Hut was a disaster. Gary's mind was elsewhere – part of it pulled towards The Lion, part to Harry's caravan and part towards Beth. This left little for answering detailed questions from the Bible.

'What's the matter with you, man?' asked Darren,

furious. Darren enjoyed studying the Bible and was the captain of the YPF's formidable quiz team. He enjoyed winning and his team always won. But not this time: the Statham Road Baptists beat them. Gary had let the side down and knew it.

Beth who had watched the competition came to cheer him up. 'It's only a game,' she said. 'Nobody cares except Darren.'

'And me,' Gary answered quietly.

Piers watched them sitting in silence, drinking cans of Pepsi, as Darren and Claire complained to him about Gary's lack of concentration. It was the first time the boy had represented the YPF and – if they had their way – it would be the last.

'Leave it to me,' said Piers.

He walked over to Gary and Beth. He laid a hand on the boy's shoulder. 'Bad luck, Gary. Your heart wasn't in it.'

Gary miserably agreed. Piers believed Gary was still upset by his mother's visit the day before; he had no idea of their visit to Harry. He called to the youngsters from The Ark. 'I'm taking Gary and Beth in the van. The rest of you can find your own way.' There was a storm of protest but Piers grinned. 'It's historic,' he said. 'I'm driving Christians to The Lion!' The YPF groaned good-naturedly and Piers turned back to Gary. 'You've got some sorting-out to do,' he said softly. 'I'm taking you home.'

Although Piers and Beth had been content to wait outside in the van, Eileen insisted they sit by the bright fire in the empty lounge bar. Piers politely refused her offer of a drink but Beth accepted a glass of cider and they sat either side of the fire, talking quietly. Derek sullenly agreed to look after both bars while his wife and son talked privately in the kitchen. Knowing Gary's present feelings towards him, the man felt angry and rejected. From time to time he walked from the public bar to survey Piers and Beth with a calm look of contempt which they were careful not to return. They nodded politely whenever they met his glance.

Once Gary began opening his heart to Eileen he found it was hard to stop. He told her of his visit to the caravan. He told her about Harry's grandson Kent and his friend Eddie. He told her about the Vincent Street Baths but gave few details and never mentioned the basement of the disused school at all.

As Beth and Piers waited, they were joined by a middle-aged man, well wrapped up against the chilly evening, who wished them good evening and sat at the counter. After a minute or two, unable to see Derek round the angle of the bar counters, he rapped a coin against the beer pumps for service. Derek heard the man, drank the whisky he had just poured and walked behind the lounge bar counter ready to take offence. 'Yes?'

The man smiled pleasantly. 'Evening,' he said. 'And a cold one at that.'

Derek called to Piers and Beth. 'I've got a paying customer here who says he's cold. Get those chairs back so he can see something of that fire.'

There was an embarrassed silence. The man protested. 'No, please. It's fine.'

Derek turned to him. 'This is my house. I do what I please. What can I get you?'

The man ordered a low-alcohol beer which Derek poured and placed before him. He took the money, delivered change and stalked away to the other bar. Out of sight, he poured himself another large whisky.

'That bloody Holy Joe!' he muttered to himself.

The stranger turned to Piers and Beth. 'Sorry about that,' he said, meaning it.

In the kitchen Gary was feeling easier. Eileen had assured him that Derek had learned his lesson and was no danger to her safety. He was far more concerned with trying to hold on to his few remaining customers. It was the sort of conversation they should have had a long time ago. Eileen felt its value too.

'Cup of tea?' she asked. 'Or do you want to join your friends in the lounge?'

Gary still had much to explain to her about his new life. 'Tea here, please,' he said. 'Mum? Thanks.'

Derek leaned on the lounge counter and watched Piers and Beth intently. They were careful – for Gary's sake – to avoid his bleary gaze. Beth had finished her drink. To be helpful she took the empty glass to the counter.

'There you go,' she said politely.

'You want another?'

Beth hesitated, not wanting to offend Derek by refusing. She thought it would be friendly to accept his offer. 'All right,' she smiled. 'Thanks.'

Derek poured the cider. He put it before her. 'That's fifty pence.' Beth's face fell. She was embarrassed at having misunderstood.

'Sorry. I don't have any money with me.'

Piers stood at once and came to the counter digging in his pocket for change but Derek picked up the glass and threw the cider down the sink. 'If you can't pay, don't ask.'

Derek turned to the stranger who was drinking up quickly, anxious to leave the unpleasant atmosphere. 'Bunch of bloody hypocrites, they are. Quick enough to preach against an honest pub like this but you should see them grab at a free drink. You should see them in here with their pamphlets and their collecting-tins!'

'We'll wait in the van,' Piers murmured to Beth. 'Listen, Mr Byrne,' the pastor said, feeling himself begin to rise to the provocation, 'members of my church do *not* collect in pubs, we do *not* hand out pamphlets without permission and we do *not* expect anything for nothing.' He slammed down a fifty-pence coin on the counter and moved with Beth towards the door.

Derek's temper broke. 'They've turned my son

against me – this one and his Do-Gooders.' He tugged the counter flap open and barged through to stand belligerently between Piers and the way out. He swayed. 'I've talked to solicitors so watch your step.'

Piers struggled to keep his voice quiet and calm. 'Gary is sixteen. He's legally able to leave his parents' home with their permission.'

Derek shouted, 'I don't give my permission!'

'But Mrs Byrne did. She said you wouldn't contest it – under the circumstances.' Piers' accusing gaze locked on to Derek's milky eyes and Derek's breath jumped in fury. How dare this Holy Joe judge him!

He looked at Piers. 'Do you let them share a room? Share a bed?' He leered at Beth. 'How old are you, little girl? Do you let him watch?' He stumbled to the door and pulled it open. 'Get out of my house.'

Piers was white-faced with anger and embarrassment for Beth. He glared at the drunk man. He saw his fear and resentment. His anger melted and he spoke softly, in sincere regret. 'I pity you, Mr Byrne. I pity your wife and your son but most of all I pity you and ask the Lord to heal you.'

Beth screamed as Derek's head butted into Pier's face. He reeled back and almost fell, spraying blood from his nose. In a moment the stranger was between them. Beth tried to stem the flow of blood with her handkerchief.

'That's enough!' shouted the stranger, holding Derek's arms.

Gary burst into the bar with Eileen.

'You fool,' she shouted at her husband. She helped Piers into a chair.

Wide-eyed and afraid, Beth ran to Gary. He took her in his arms and tried to comfort her while his father struggled in the man's grip. 'Can't you mind your own business?' Derek shouted.

He was suddenly exhausted. For the first time he was aware of what he had done and stepped back. The stranger reached inside his coat for a wallet and angrily held out a card. 'This *is* my business,' he said.

'Thomas Partington,' the card read. 'Managing Director, Bellings Brewery.'

EIGHT

It was fortunate that one of The Hut's congregation was a doctor who hurried to The Ark as soon as Mr Turner phoned. The Turners were strongly in favour of calling the police but Piers spelled out the consequences of summoning Gary's father for assault. In any case Derek Byrne was in enough trouble with Thomas Partington.

It was midnight by the time Dr Booth had left. The nose was not broken but would be painful for a day or two and Piers would have a couple of black eyes in the morning. Dr Booth thought Piers had been lucky. Piers replied wryly that the doctor had a very strange definition of 'luck'. Piers did his best to make light of the incident for the sake of Gary. The hour at The Lion had been a fiasco and the boy felt entirely responsible. When Dr Booth and everybody else had left Piers' living-room, with much hugging and promises of prayer, John had made coffee and a deep silence fell.

'Better get to bed then,' murmured John, reaching for his mug.

The three of them looked at silent Gary, head in his hands on the sofa. Beth sat at his side with an arm across his shoulders. 'Gary?' she said softly.

Gary looked up at her. His life was out of his control. One moment he was down under the heels of Kent Bailey and Eddie Watts and the next he was up, secure in love and faith. And now this. 'I just think I ought to phone my mother again,' he whispered.

Beth squeezed his arm. 'Better to leave them.'

Piers reached for the Paracetamol bottle and shook two tablets into his hand. 'Beth's right. There's nothing you can do – not yet.' He swallowed the pain-killers with the last of his coffee.

'Piers – I don't know what to say to you.'

They looked at Gary with understanding.

'I don't know what to do.' His eyes filled with tears.

Beth took the initiative. 'Come on,' she said, standing. ''Night, Piers. 'Night, John.'

She drew him to his feet and they left the room together. Through the open door John and Piers watched them climb the stairs to the floor above.

'It's very late, you two,' called Piers quietly.

If they heard him they didn't show it. John glanced over and knew the pastor was not pleased.

'More coffee, Piers?' he said.

John was right. Piers was not pleased but he pulled his attention back from the staircase and forced a smile. 'Why not? Thanks, John.'

'Lock the door,' said Beth quietly. She drew back the bed cover. She looked very seriously at him. He looked away.

'I don't know . . .'

'Lock the door,' she repeated firmly.

Gary turned the key slowly. 'Never done this before,' he whispered, scared, tired, excited.

Beth came to Gary and lifted his arms round her neck. She circled his waist and drew him close. She kissed him and began drawing up his shirt from his waistband.

John returned from locking the front door and checking the lights. Piers was exactly as he had left him, silent in his chair.

'Is this the first time, John?' he asked.

John was uneasy. 'How do you mean?'

'Beth and Gary – spending the night together.'

John coughed nervously. 'They're probably just saying good-night.'

'I asked you a question, John.' Piers' voice was

cold. A late-night bus passed along Victoria Road.

'I don't know,' he said. 'Yes. I think so. I mean – I've never heard them before.'

He sneaked a look at Piers' face. The bruising was beginning to show. It gave his features an ugly twist. John finished his coffee as quickly as he could and left.

Gary slipped into the narrow bed in the dark and felt himself held tight. He felt overwhelmed with Beth's care and concern for him. It began to smooth everything else – no matter how terrible – into the background, for the moment at least. They kissed for a long time.

'I love you more than anything or anybody in the whole world,' he gasped.

Beth made no reply and Gary wondered if he had said the wrong thing. At last she spoke, in a low monotone. 'Don't say that.'

'I love you,' said Gary.

Beth pulled him against her. 'Hold me tight,' she whispered.

Piers stood at his door and heard John's steps creak softly along the top landing to his room. He felt old and exhausted. His left cheek was throbbing and he had a sharp headache.

He walked across the room to open the window and breathe the sharp spring air. The road was quiet now, though he could hear a train shunting a mile away in the station. Piers turned to look at the only picture he possessed, the only one in the room, a beautifully framed modern picture of Jesus, specially painted for Piers by a friend.

'Is this really what you want?' he asked quietly. 'Is this the only reason you brought them here?'

He drew a chair in front of the picture and sat in silence contemplating his Lord, needing advice, guidance, support.

★ ★ ★

Gary woke to a silent house and bright sun warming the thin curtains. He lay for a while dazed with heavy, dreamless sleep until he slowly raised his wrist and focused on his watch: ten o'clock – TEN O'CLOCK? Gary sat up with a shock. Late for college. He'd already missed economics. He jumped out of bed and began dressing quickly. His mood was nervous and high. He didn't know how he felt about the wonderful and frightening thing that had happened; the only thing he was sure of was Beth. On the landing he listened for washing-up or hoovering or anything to give away her whereabouts. Nothing. He took the four steps to her door, tapped and went in. The room was empty. Bare. There was nothing to show it had ever been used. Looking out of the window he saw a space where the 2CV was always parked.

PART FOUR

The BUNKER

ONE

Gary tugged his anorak collar higher and wondered where all the cars had gone. In two hours it would be dark and it had been a quarter of an hour since he had seen a vehicle of any sort. At that moment a car appeared in the distance and Gary waited to see what direction it would take at this roundabout in the middle of nowhere. He was prepared to revise his plans and even accept a lift back to the M1 which he had been fool enough to leave an hour and a half earlier. At least on the motorway he would have a good chance of heading south, to Junction 11, near Banbury and seventeen miles from Brackley.

The Sierra slowed down for the roundabout. The driver glanced across at the boy, cold and hunched at the side of the road, but took the road north, to Leicester. Gary watched the car out of sight and his spirits dropped. He was tired and hungry. He had eaten nothing all day except half the chocolate bar from the garage where he had studied a road atlas. Gary pulled off a glove and scrabbled in his pocket for the rest of the chocolate.

Was the journey a good idea? He only knew it was something he must do. The Turners had been off-hand with him. They had looked at him with tight disapproving faces. No – they didn't know where Beth had gone. No – they didn't know when she had left. No – they didn't know if she would be coming back.

He heard an engine in the distance and turned to where the road curved. At least it was travelling in the right direction. 'Please, Lord?' he asked urgently.

A tractor casually rolled over the crest of a hill a few fields away to begin ploughing.

'Very funny, Lord,' Gary thought. Ah well, a joke was better than nothing. There had been nothing jokey about the conversation he had had with John at college. At first there was no conversation; his friend could hardly meet his eyes.

'John, this is me speaking – Gary. What's the matter? Why won't you talk to me.'

'I am talking to you.'

'You know what I mean. Where's Beth?'

John shifted uneasily. At last he shrugged. 'Sorry, mate. It just couldn't go on. Piers thought – well, we all did – '

'What's it got to do with Piers or you or anyone?'

John dropped his eyes in embarrassment. The college bell rang for the beginning of the session before lunch. He took an envelope from the inside pocket of his coat. 'Piers told me to give you this.' Gary took it gingerly, knowing it could only contain bad news; he did not want to open it. John looked round at students hurrying towards the double doors. 'Are you coming to economics?' he asked lamely.

'I love her, John.' Gary's eyes filled with tears but he was not ashamed. Behind them the students chattered and laughed.

John dropped his eyes. 'I know,' he muttered.

Gary tore the envelope open and read Piers' letter carefully while John hung about, feeling unable to go. When Gary finished he looked up at his friend and shook his head in puzzled regret. John still would not meet his gaze and Gary did not need to ask if he knew what was in the letter.

Suddenly Gary turned on his heel and walked angrily away to his bike. 'See you, John,' he muttered.

'Right. See you tonight.'

Gary turned. 'No,' he snapped. 'I'm going home for a few days. I need to be away from all you caring Christians at The Ark. I need time to think.' He strode away.

'It's all for the best, Gary,' John called wretchedly behind him.

At the roundabout Gary reread Piers' letter for the fourth time.

My dear Gary,

I have been praying all night about you and Beth. The Lord has told me what to do.

When Beth turned up with her difficult questions she forced us to confront our own beliefs. At the time I thought that was the only reason she had been sent. Now I know the Lord had another task for her – to lead you to us. Caring for you and solving your problems has united the YPF in a wonderful way and I thank God for it.

Now it is time for Beth to leave. The relationship between you is not helpful or healthy. You will know what Saint Paul tells us about sexual love – if we are to concentrate on God's work (and I am sure He has sent you to us for that purpose) then we must allow no complications or distractions to stand in the way. You will not thank me for telling Beth she should leave us but you must see the days ahead as a test of your obedience to God. I look forward to talking and praying with you tonight. We all love and care for you very much.

Ever your shepherd,

Piers

How dare he? Pastor Piers the shepherd – as if Gary were some stupid beast needing to be kept safely in line with all the other woolly halfwits. How dare he? How could they? And how could she just go without a word?

'Do you want a lift or don't you?' said the driver of a white Honda Prelude purring at his side. 'And if you do, get in. I can't stay here for ever.'

Stammering thanks and apologies Gary picked up his bag and climbed into the passenger seat. 'Where are you making for?' the driver asked. Gary pulled the passenger door shut and reached for the seat belt. 'Banbury,' he said.

The driver glanced in his mirrors and drew away from the side of the road. 'Can't take you all the way,' he said. 'I can drop you somewhere quite close. I'm making for Oxford but I've got to call at Brackley. That's not far from Banbury. Is that all right?'

'That's great, thanks,' said Gary, stuffing Piers' letter into his pocket and settling back in his seat to enjoy the ride. 'Thanks, Lord,' he added in his head as the man put his foot down and the Prelude accelerated smoothly away from the roundabout.

Gary said goodbye to the driver in the windy town square at Brackley. Now that he had arrived he was not sure what to do and it was after five o'clock. He looked across to The Crown Inn, wondering how much bed and breakfast would cost – more than he had in his pocket probably, though he would be able to take more from his savings account in the morning if there were a branch of the Halifax here.

He saw a bed and breakfast sign outside a neat-looking house on the edge of the square and decided he would stay there – so long as they didn't ask him too many questions. Would they think it strange for a boy of his age to be travelling on his own? Eileen and Derek would: they'd check with the police. Gary fought back his fears. The Ark thought he was at The Lion and his parents thought he was at The Ark. Nobody would be looking for him.

It was cold but Gary was glad. The air in the car had been stuffy and Gary needed waking up. He needed to be sharp. He also needed food. He walked over to a newsagent's shop to buy more chocolate and a can of drink.

He swallowed the Mars and Cola in the shelter of the old stone market hall. The clock above him chimed five-fifteen and he began to make plans. He knew Beth's surname – Garnett – and that she lived near Brackley.

He was excited to think of her so near. In a corner of the square was a phone box with a phone book miraculously in one piece. He strained his eyes to read the small grey print. Gary counted eleven Garnetts and one Garnet. He hurried to catch the newsagent before he closed and changed two pounds for twenty ten-pence coins.

'Garnett A.C., 15 Lower Castle St, Banbury.' After sixteen rings Gary asked a breathless man if he could speak to Beth. The man wheezed that Gary had the wrong number and put the phone down. 'Garnett C.J., 16 Goodwyn Avenue, Brackley.' No reply. Gary tried again. No reply. 'Garnett Maj H.T., The Grange, Turweston.' A woman answered almost at once with a highly polished voice. She had never heard of Beth. 'Garnett Antiques, Queenswood Drive, Banbury.' An answer-phone told Gary the shop was closed until the morning and to speak clearly after the bleep if he wished to leave a message. He didn't. 'Garnett K., The Mill School, Westbury.' Beth said, 'Yes, hello, The Mill School.' Gary panicked and put the phone down.

'How long you going to be?' A woman with a small pale child rapped hard on the glass, breaking through his shock. Gary mumbled apologies and stumbed out into the wind. 'About time too,' said the woman, pushing the miserable child past Gary into the shelter of the box.

Gary made himself talk. 'Please. Do you know a place called Westbury?'

'Out on the Buckingham road.' The door was almost shut.

'How far please?'

The woman opened the door again and peered at Gary suspiciously. 'How should I know?' she said. 'Two miles? Three?' The child tugged at her coat but curiosity had the better of her now. She looked Gary up and down. 'What d'you want to know for anyway?'

Gary shrugged, working out a lie, but then the sad

child tugged at the woman again and she turned to the phone, giving Gary one last furious look as if the blame for the dark, the cold, her grizzling child and life in general should be laid at his feet. Gary ran back to the newsagent's but the shop was dark. He was crossing a road making for The Crown and further information when he saw the sign – 'Buckingham 6'. Gary didn't think twice. 'Thanks, Lord,' he said, walking briskly into the night.

TWO

After five minutes Gary had left the town behind him and the pavement ran out at a deserted industrial estate. He shifted his bag to the other hand and concentrated on keeping up a good pace, grateful that the wind was behind him. There was very little traffic on the minor road and nothing stopped for him. It was early evening: everyone wanted to be home. Home.

Gary wondered how things were at The Lion. The pub would be open now and there would be a customer or two in the main bar. His father would be reading the evening paper at the counter while his mother watched the television news. He felt bad about deserting and deceiving his parents but last night had changed his life. He remembered the scene in the lounge bar – Piers bleeding, Beth scared, his father shouting. He remembered the despair of his mother, and her quiet strength. Too complicated. Too much. He remembered his room at The Ark. He needed Beth.

He pulled his thoughts back to the present. A busy road barred his way and he hurried across, dodging a fan of spray from a long-distance coach. Soon he was striding towards Buckingham in the darkness again and his mind began to race.

What had happened at The Ark while he slept? He went over it all yet again.

After he and Beth had made love they had talked for a while – he had done most of the talking – and he had fallen deeply asleep. He did not know if Beth had returned to her own room then or if she had quietly got up at the usual time and decided to let him sleep on. Whichever it was, that was when Piers would have talked to her with John and Frankie at his side, all full of love and care but anxious to let Beth know she had outstayed her welcome now that she was taking a different sort of interest in the YPF pet lamb ('ever your shepherd'!). Gary hoped she had flared up and told them a few home truths. He wished she had left him a message of some sort but it was just like Beth to pack up there and then. More direct, more honest. Their night together had been so overwhelming for Gary and so wonderful, so right, that he could not believe God found it unhelpful or unhealthy, as Piers did. If God disapproved, why had he found Gary a direct lift to Brackley and helped him discover Beth within twenty minutes of searching?

Twenty minutes later, with the same thoughts chasing round his brain, Gary saw lights in the distance and came across the Westbury sign at the side of the road. The lights turned out to be from a pub called The Reindeer whose landlady came into the street to point out the impressive gateway to The Mill School. As he walked quickly past the silent houses Gary cursed his panic in the Brackley phone box. He wished he knew how Beth would feel about their all-important meeting that was only minutes away. He put all doubts from his mind. He was in love. He held on firmly to that as he walked up the school drive.

'What the hell do you think you're doing here?' Beth broke off to call a bad-tempered 'Yes?' to a knock on the door and a small boy came into the surgery. The boy carefully closed the door behind him and glanced at Gary. The child shifted from foot to foot. 'Please, matron, I feel sick.' He looked anxiously at Beth.

'What am I supposed to do about it?'

The boy was dressed in a grey sweater, grey shirt, grey shorts and a pair of grey socks. The only things he wore which were not grey were his tie (red) and shoes (black). Beth got unwillingly to her feet. 'Come here.'

The boy obediently stood before her and she laid

her hand on his forehead. 'You're all right,' she said brusquely. 'It's your own fault. You must have pigged yourself stupid at tea.' The boy shook his head in strong denial. 'Anyway, I'm not letting you off prep. What's your name?'

'Edwards, please, matron.'

'Go back down and get on with your work, Edwards. See me again before you go to bed.'

The boy shifted his balance from foot to foot. Gary thought that his colour was beginning to match his outfit.

'Can I have a drink of water, please, matron?'

'You can get a drink of water downstairs. Don't bother me now. I'm busy.'

The child thanked her politely and left.

There was another long silence and Gary stared at her in dumb misery. He could not believe how different she was in her formal blue dress and white overall coat instead of jeans and a sweater. Her hair was fixed tight on her head, not flying freely as he had always known it. She looked older.

'You were about to explain what you're doing here.'

Gary spoke in a whisper, almost in shame. 'I needed to see you.'

A bell sounded somewhere in the house and she glanced at a watch pinned to her dress.

'I have to be on duty in ten minutes.'

Gary gestured hopelessly towards her dress and round the rest of the room. 'I didn't know about any of this.'

'It's nothing to do with you. When I'm home I have to help out where they need me. That's all.' Her eyes narrowed. 'Was that you who phoned here earlier?'

He nodded. This felt terrible. Everything was wrong. She was a different person and was making him into a different person too. 'I love you, Beth,' he said.

Beth sighed heavily. 'Yes,' she said. 'I know. That's

the trouble. Why do you think I left?'

She saw his face crumple. 'Listen,' she said calmly. 'This is how it was.'

She told him how she had been ready to move from The Ark by the end of the year. The YPF had lost all interest. Then Gary had appeared on the scene. 'You were different from the others. Not so sure of yourself. Vulnerable. And you're quite good-looking.' So Beth decided to stay on for a week or two.

She had been excited by Gary's confrontation with Derek. She smiled without humour. 'You'll understand why when you meet my father.' So Gary came to live at The Ark and, like the rest, Beth had been appalled about the bullying – and intrigued too. 'You seemed to accept it as if you were only getting what you deserved. You needed somebody to protect you – from the YPF creeps as well as Kent Bailey and Eddie Watts.' After their satisfying defeat she had gloried in the emotional celebrations. 'One of the best times of my life,' she said. 'Yes. Really.' There was a pause and her face softened and he briefly saw the girl he loved.

'I love you, Beth,' he said again.

She looked him steadily in the eyes. 'But then you changed. You became just like the rest of them. Boring. So sure of everything. Spending every moment at the dreary little Hut. Shining with goodness. Boring boring boring.' Beth saw the hurt. 'Sorry,' she said softly. 'You really shouldn't have come here.'

Gary shook his head disbelievingly and Beth moved to a large cupboard where she began checking medicines. 'When you weren't being virtuous,' she said, 'you were feeling sorry for yourself. I warned you about that. That's the trouble with men. They're either cocksure of everything or grizzling with self-pity.' She closed the cupboard door and turned to Gary. 'Just like you are now,' she added.

Gary knew the subject had to be raised. 'But last night – '

She cut roughly across his words. 'Last night you were soggy with self-pity. So was Piers.'

'I mean . . . later. Afterwards.'

Beth knew what he meant. She sat on a hard upright chair and looked directly at him. 'That was a mistake,' she murmured. Gary was angry. He shouted, 'No. It was . . .' He searched for the right word and felt tears in his eyes. '. . . Wonderful.'

Beth held her level gaze upon him. 'Not wonderful,' she said in a strange voice. She turned her attention to the gas fire and crouched down to adjust it. 'It was all right. Not as good as Darren but better than John.'

There was total silence. Gary felt as if he were dying. Beth rose from the fire. Heavy steps scuffed the wooden stairs and the door suddenly flew open.

'Who is this?'

The man who had entered was tall. His face was lined and tanned. He was immaculately dressed in a blazer, white shirt and sharply creased dark trousers. He wore a regimental tie and his shoes shone like glass. Beth looked blankly up at him with an expression that was almost insolent.

'Someone I happen to know. That's all. Nothing to do with you.' Beth turned her head towards Gary. 'This is Major Garnett,' Beth drawled, emphasising 'Major'. 'Headmaster of this fine little school.'

It seemed impossible for Gary to do or say anything. In any case the major took no notice of him. 'Your mother's just had to see to Ben Edwards,' he complained to Beth. 'The child's been sick in the living-room. He says he came to you but you sent him away.'

Beth kept her face blank and said nothing. Major Garnett flicked his eyes towards Gary. 'We'll talk about it over dinner,' he muttered to her.

'I might not be in for dinner.'

The major glared at her. He clenched his fists. 'But you said you'd be matron-on-duty tonight.' Father and daughter stared at each other. 'People pay a great deal of money to send their boys here,' he snapped. 'They deserve consideration.'

'So do I,' Beth snapped back.

Gary looked from one to the other. Like Ben Edwards, he felt sick. He stood suddenly and reached for his wet anorak steaming on a radiator. They turned as he picked up his bag and made for the door. 'Wait here,' Beth said to her father.

She followed Gary through the door, closing it behind her. 'Where are you going?' she said. 'What are you going to do?' He shrugged, just wanting to be outside in the soothing dark. Beth put her arms round him but he didn't move. 'It got complicated,' she whispered. 'I warned you about that.' She kissed his cheek and let Gary go. They looked at each other for a few seconds. 'Last night was my going-away present to you,' she said softly. 'Something to remember me by. But don't think it was the beginning of anything, Gary. It was the end.'

The bell rang again and noise filled the school immediately – deafening and hysterical like wild animals. Footsteps, laughter, screams and shouts filled the air. Gary was too numb to panic. Instead, he nodded farewell and pressed downstairs against a rising swarm of shouting children. A few looked at him curiously but most ignored him. He felt worthless, invisible. Nothing.

Gary fought his way through the frantic upstairs rush without looking back. He needed to be out in the darkness, needed to be alone with his thoughts. Also he was going to cry and didn't want these screeching children to see him.

THREE

Much later, when he was asked, Gary could not really remember the next few hours. He remembered walking back towards Brackley in a daze. He recalled a lorry driver asking him if he was feeling all right and warning him not to be sick in the cab. He seemed to think that the driver dropped him at a major crossroads. A woman in a van stuck in Gary's mind, too, but all he knew for sure was that some time after midnight he was leaving a car at College Hill, back where he had started. All the rest was a blur.

Gary sat on a bench outside the café at the top of the hill and began to fall asleep. He had spent most of the return journey sleeping and wondered what was going to happen to him next. He would never return to The Ark. He considered The Lion or Harry's caravan but they were far away and his strength and will-power were fading. In any case he could not face his parents yet and remembered Harry's angry coldness when he and Beth had visited him.

Beth. Every time he thought about her he wanted to cry. Now that his journey was definitely over, the sobs came immediately and water streamed down his cheeks. He searched his jeans pocket for a handkerchief as his nose began to run. He could not stop. He abandoned himself to this immense grief, careless of what anybody might think who saw him.

But when he heard happy voices approaching he suddenly did not want to be seen. It was a private torment. He saw the group coming up the hill, boys and girls wrapped round each other. Gary got to his feet and took his bag. He didn't even think as he stumbled between the shop and café behind him to the overgrown

Art College path. When he forced open the side door and squeezed into the derelict school he immediately felt safe. With a shock Gary realised it was like coming home.

He wandered through the assembly hall. In the fitful moonlight the echoing space was magical. Gary walked round the edge of the hall, scuffling through the rubble, enchanted. The door to the corridor hung on one hinge. Gary pushed past and stopped.

A distant street light, screened by trees, was angling flickering orange against a patch of wall where a large square frame had once held a heavy picture or notice board. The screws had snapped, the joints had separated and most of the frame had fallen among the debris and dust but a crosspiece was left on the wall – a rough cross, skewed at an angle. A cross.

Gary stood gazing up at it for a long time. It became important to straighten the cross and he stepped over rubble to reach up but the moment he touched it the final screw cracked and the wood fell from the wall. Staggering forward, dropping his bag, Gary involuntarily tried to catch it but his foothold on the rubble failed and he felt himself falling. When feeling and consciousness returned he thought he had broken his leg and there was a deep cut behind his right ear which would rack his head.

It took Gary a long time to drag his bag and the cross to the top of the basement steps where somebody had sprayed 'The Bunker' on the door. Safely inside, he pulled his sleeping-bag from the sports grip and shoved the smashed furniture aside to create a level space. He propped up the cross where he could see it. He was beginning to feel very strange. His head and leg hurt badly and his tiredness and despair seemed to create an emptiness inside him so total that he didn't know how much longer he would be able to carry on. Also he felt sick – like Ben Edwards who had wanted water. Gary forced himself to his feet. There was a grimy sink next to the showers whose tap was very stiff but Gary managed two turns and water trickled out. In the dimness Gary could not see the colour. He cupped his hand and sucked. He drank two mouthfuls.

Energy had almost gone. He concentrated on tugging off his trainers and crawling into his sleeping-bag. It had been the longest and most dreadful day of his life and he was too tired to weep, too tired even to think of Beth – or anything. He listened to the building as it creaked and groaned. Gary felt wonderfully secure. The Bunker represented a simpler life. He had not had the power to refuse the torments that Kent Bailey and Eddie Watts had wished upon him. Like his fall in the corridor it had not been his fault. There had been nothing he could do about it.

Kent Bailey and Eddie Watts. Gary waited for the wall but nothing happened. It was another loss. The Panic Wall had trapped him behind it but it had been a protection too. Gary closed his eyes. It was his last thought before exhaustion gained him and even when the banshee of fighting cats erupted, his eyes flickered but he did not wake.

When next he opened his sore eyes, it took him a long time to realise where he was. He lay stupified in his sleeping-bag, too feeble to move, and listened to the monotonous churning of a cement mixer somewhere near. He tried to frame a decision about what should be done but his mind was slow and sludgy and pulled his thoughts apart before he could join them up. He was soon dreaming again and although the dreams were vivid and brief he could not remember any when he woke.

Now there were schoolchildren playing games on the fields behind the building and he listened to their high excited voices with a sort of serene love. 'Suffer the little children to come unto me,' he whispered and the next time he woke up they had. The smokers were in

The Bunker: he heard the murmur of their voices and their showy exhalations. Gary smiled to think of them so close. He would like to have spoken with them but knew he would scare them. He must have dozed off then for when he woke again it was dark.

Gary lay perfectly still trying to judge the time without having to move his arm and look at his watch which was somehow a problem. He could hear the distant drone of traffic but all around him there was complete silence. Gary needed the school toilets, wherever they were, and gently eased his arms from the sleeping-bag. He dimly remembered finding water in a tap and knew this could mean a flushing toilet. He slowly began to draw himself from the soft comfort of his cocoon.

He was immediately in pain. It throbbed through his head, jabbed in his leg and gripped his limbs in a general stiffness so that Gary gasped and froze, unwilling to move again until the pain was over. Out in the air he noticed his clothes were damp with sweat and when he wiped a hand across his hot forehead his fingertips came near the cut behind his ear and he winced at the soreness. He tried hard to put his thoughts in order but it was still too difficult. 'Lord?' he whispered, puzzled. 'What's happening?'

He found toilets next door to The Bunker. Although the seats had gone and the cubicles were without doors he was relieved to find they were grubby rather than unclean. Gary pulled a chain experimentally but nothing happened. And then a break-through: his mind at last clicked into gear and began working. He located the water tap for the whole system in the first cubicle and picked up a rusty six-inch nail in the corridor to lever it open. Soon water was popping and gurgling in the pipes. There was no paper but Gary shuffled back into The Bunker pleased to find a suitable use for Piers' letter. When he finished, the cistern flushed so noisily he was sure nobody outside could ignore it and was relieved not to hear it refill – there were still four other cubicles with full tanks. One of the basins provided a trickle of red-brown water to wash his hands but that was the limit of his recovery. He began to feel dizzy and the next thing he knew, he was waking up in his sleeping-bag, sweating and aching, in shorts and socks, the rest of his clothes neatly folded over a three-legged chair at his side. The evening coldness of The Bunker instantly chilled the film of sweat on his body and he began to shiver. He reached for his clothes and pulled them on as quickly as he could. They were damp and very cold. His teeth began chattering – he could not make them stop – and then his shoulders shivered, then his thighs. His whole body began to twitch. Gary clambered up and hugged himself. He stamped his feet. No good. He sat down and wrapped the sleeping-bag round his shoulders, pulling his legs tight to his chest and linking fingers round his knees. Gary moaned and rocked, waiting for warmth. 'Lord,' he groaned. 'How long, O Lord? How long?' Something must happen soon. 'Show me a sign,' he shouted. 'I don't know what you want.'

'Gary?' Somebody was shaking him by the shoulder. 'Gary – it's all right.' His eyes focused on his tiny room at The Ark and the cheap curtains with the sun shining through. He gazed up bewildered at Beth, looking anxiously down at him. She kissed him very gently on the lips. 'You've had a bad dream. It's all right.' She kissed him again. 'Close your eyes.' He shut his eyes. A dream. It was a dream. He was so grateful. Beth slid beneath the bedclothes to stretch her cool body against his.

'Gary!' His eyes snapped open on his mother in the doorway. Shame and embarrassment caught his breath and he glanced quickly to his side. No Beth. He could hear the clock of Saint Barnabas striking. He gazed round. He was in his room at The Lion. 'It's all right,' Eileen smiled, laying a cool hand across his brow.

'You've just had a bad dream. Breakfast in ten minutes. All right?'

Gary nodded and sank back into his pillows but when next he woke it was to the squealing of the fighting cats. He smelled the dry-wet concrete of The Bunker and stared into the darkness, scared to let himself be fooled by dreams again. 'Tell me what you want,' he shouted to God desperately. 'Why is this happening to me?'

As his temperature steadily rose Gary slid more and more easily between dreams and reality. He was not surprised to see The Bunker ceiling descending and the walls pressing in and soon discovered the only way to halt them was by grinding his teeth so hard that his jaws ached. As long as he kept his teeth crushed tight together the walls and ceiling stayed at bay; if his concentration lapsed – even for a second – they were moving again and he was in trouble. 'Lord?' he moaned. And then the black muzzle of a dog was six inches from his face. Gary tried hard to decide if it was a dream and hissed at the dog which barked furiously and drove in to nip him. Gary lashed out but the dog snapped at the fleshy part of his arm above the elbow at the same time as a man's angry voice shouted outside. 'Winston!' The dog froze and turned its head to The Bunker's steps.

'Winston! Come here! Winston!'

The dog bounded up the steps without a glance back. The whole incident had taken less than a minute but left Gary with a pumping heart and aching head as well as the bite on his arm. He reached cautiously to touch the other tender area, behind his ear. It was swollen and hot. Gary wriggled deep into the sleeping-bag and willed himself asleep.

Sometime during the next few hours Gary was sick. This was unexpected for it had been a long time since he had eaten the Mars bar at Brackley and he tried to work out what he had been doing there as he stood shakily at the sink to swill his mouth and drink the contaminated water. His body was aching and he had dreamed a dog had bitten his arm but yet there really was a bitemark and smear of blood. Gary began to feel very afraid. Things were out of control so he stood unsteadily in the middle of The Bunker and waited for the next thing to happen.

Everything he had done had turned disastrously wrong so he waited for what would come next. There was no point in praying. He had been abandoned. His parents had been happy to hand him over to The Ark but Piers and the YPF had not wanted him any more than Beth had. 'My God, my God, why hast thou forsaken me?' rang in his muzzy mind like a cracked continuous bell. The spring day was turning into frosty night and he started shivering. Dizziness returned with the familiar sickness, fever and headache. Gary was nothing now, worthless, and knew what must be done. It took time but at last he managed to walk unsteadily to where the cross leaned against the wall and carry it carefully to The Bunker steps. Gary fetched the long nail which he had used to turn the toilet tap and held it with the fingertips of his left hand so that the point was sharp in his left palm. He laid the back of the hand on the cross and reached for the half-brick he had put ready. He slammed the brick down on the head of the nail.

This time it was different. This time it was real. Gary screamed as the blunt point of the nail punched through his flesh and pain drove everything else from his mind. He felt it roll up his arm in a sharp poisonous tide and as the whole of his body became submerged he passed the point where it could be suffered any longer and blacked out.

He blacked out again unfixing the nail from the wood and could not face drawing it out of his hand. By the time he had done all he could, the pain had begun to ebb and Gary was marooned, half-numb and half-burning, rocking and distraught in the furthest corner of The Bunker.

The scuffling steps through the corridor's rubbish penetrated Gary's shell of pain but raised no hopes. He wasn't convinced the steps were real. Then the door was shoved open and Kent Bailey walked in.

The basement was a disappointment to Kent. In his imagination The Bunker had been large and dramatic but he saw only a small gloomy cellar cluttered with broken desks. And it stank. It was a mistake to come and he didn't know why he felt the need. He guessed that losing Eddie, his best friend since primary school, had something to do with it. Being on your own was no fun.

Kent Bailey's heart jumped when he heard the movement in the corner. He was scared of mice and rats and half-turned back towards the door. But a bigger shape than a rat was moving from the shadows. Kent drew a sharp breath and his heart began thumping. He took another step towards the door before the shape emerged from the darkness and he saw it was a man, some tramp or wino – that's why the place stank. The boy relaxed. 'You stink,' Kent Bailey called experimentally to the shambling figure. Yes, he thought, it's definitely a drunk.

Gary packed all his concentration into forcing one foot in front of the other, careful not to jar his arm and anxious for his balance. He was grateful for this intervention. Now he knew who he was, where he was and what was expected. At last life was simple and straightforward again. Gary was relieved to see the boy with grey eyes and edged painfully towards the security of the third locker from the end of the row – the one with the door. He felt himself shining and smiled to himself.

Gary stepped delicately through the orange glow of a distant street light and Kent Bailey instantly knew him and was shocked. The Byrne kid was shambling like an old man; he must be on drugs or drink. Kent Bailey stared at his grotesque progress as Gary reached the locker and turned. 'It's all right,' Gary whispered, seeing his shock and nodding encouragingly. 'I never told anyone. Nobody knows.' He concentrated on opening the locker door and Kent Bailey suddenly realised what was happening.

'What d'you think you're doing?' he shouted as he ran horrified to Gary who backed away in fear. Kent stopped at once, not wanting to scare him. 'You're bloody off your head!' he gasped.

Gary considered this and nodded seriously. He whispered so quietly that Kent could only just hear him.

'Help me.'

The first and most obvious thing Kent Bailey noticed was that Gary was shaking with cold. He quickly pulled off his anorak and draped it across Gary's shoulders as he stood in complaisant silence. Kent screwed up his eyes and stared into the shadows for a place where Gary could rest. He saw the sleeping-bag in the tangle of broken desks and led Gary towards it. 'You asked for it,' he muttered indignantly. 'You really asked for it.'

Kent kicked chairs and desks away to make a bigger space. The shock was beginning to lessen and he began thinking what he should do next. 'What's the problem?' he demanded. 'What's the matter with you?' He noticed Gary held a hand behind his back and was instantly wary – he could have a knife, a hammer, some sort of weapon. Kent Bailey backed off, ready to move very fast. 'Okay,' he said quietly, 'so what have you got behind your back? No tricks, right?'

Slowly and with great care Gary drew his hand from behind his back and held it out to Kent, raising his eyes, half-coy and half-terrified at what he was showing. 'Who done this to you?' Kent breathed. He could hardly believe the horror of it.

'I don't know,' said Gary, sobbing.

Kent helped Gary into a sitting position on the sleeping-bag. He found the boy's anorak and wrapped it round his body. His mind raced over what should be done. The hand was a mess; Gary Byrne was a mess and had to go to hospital. But that would mean difficult questions which might lead back to The Bunker on a different occasion. Kent licked his lips nervously as he watched Gary hold the wrist of his torn hand tight against his chest. I could go now, he thought. I could just leave him. He's delirious and would forget I was ever here. I could dial 999 from the box at the top of College Hill. Gary read his thoughts.

'Don't leave me.'

Kent looked guiltily into Gary's eyes. 'You got to go to hospital,' he said. 'You understand? I got to go and phone the ambulance.' He saw Gary's face tighten in distress. 'Don't leave me,' Gary repeated, more frightened. 'Please.' Gary leaned back, exhausted.

Even in the strange basement lighting his colour looked terrible: Kent had never seen anyone so sick. He slid into a sitting position at Gary's side. 'You're sick, man. You can't stay here all night.'

There was silence. Kent was beginning to feel the cold too and wrapped his arms round himself. 'How long you been down here?' he shivered. Gary shook his head: he had no idea. 'Lucky for you I turned up then.'

Gary brought his concentration to bear on the statement and considered it very seriously. At last he nodded. 'Yes,' he said. 'It was just luck.'

Kent turned to Gary. 'Look,' he said urgently, 'I've got to get you help.' He nodded towards Gary's hand, hardly daring to look at it. 'That's serious trouble.' The horrible idea struck him again. 'Who did this to you?' He could hardly bear the direction his thoughts were leading. 'Nobody done this to you for a laugh?' he said. He lost himself in his thoughts. Was jabbing a nail through the Byrne kid's hand worse than throwing darts at his eyes?

'I've been here two days,' said Gary clearly, startling Kent Bailey. Now he was not moving and the pain was under control his mind was clearing. Gary tried hard to find the sequence of events. 'I went away then came back here. I was sick and a dog bit me.'

Gary's clarity pulled Kent's thoughts back to him. 'Why did you come down here?' he asked quietly. 'It's a poxy place. Terrible.'

Gary looked at him squarely. 'Why did *you*?' Their eyes locked. Although neither gave an answer it was as if they had come to a silent understanding. A motorbike screamed over the crest of College Hill and they heard it surge down towards Cromwell Street and fade into the distant mumble of traffic.

'Listen,' said Kent Bailey. He looked away. It was as if he were rehearsing something important and was determined to get it right. He looked back into Gary's eyes. 'It's the thrill, right? The sheer bloody thrill of it. Being in total control. Like you own the person you're doing it to, right? And like you do whatever you want, right? Like you're God. You know?'

Gary knew. In Kent's passionate explanation he recognised an echo of Piers, of Beth, even of his father. All these people needing – *needing* the thrill, needing to be God. And needing a victim to fulfil their fantasies.

'Why?' Gary whispered.

Kent was puzzled. 'I just told you.'

'No,' insisted Gary. 'I mean why do you need it?'

Kent looked away again. It was a question his parents had asked him. He had no answer. 'Why didn't you run?' he countered angrily. 'You could have fought or shouted. You didn't have to give yourself up like you did.'

Gary nodded. He and Kent Bailey were two halves of the same need. Without each other they were nothing. In the silence there was that sense of mutual acceptance again.

'Let me see that.' Kent Bailey reached for Gary's hand and held it gently. It was hot, throbbing. It must hurt like hell. He studied it and blew softly on the torn flesh. 'That any better?' he asked. 'Any help?'

It had been a long time since anybody had wanted to help Gary and his eyes filled with tears. He nodded, biting them back while Kent, embarrassed but relieved to find something helpful to do, blew softly across the wound again. It mattered more and more to him that Gary should not suffer unduly. It made nonsense of everything that had gone before and Kent knew it.

'Come on,' he said brusquely, scared that he might catch Gary's fears and cry. 'We got to get to College Hill.' Gary seemed doubtful: he knew how weak he was but Kent kneeled before him. 'We can do this, Gary. We can. Trust me?' Gary nodded and let Kent Bailey draw his good arm across his shoulders to haul him to his feet.

It was soon obvious it was going to be very hard and they were edging with difficulty from the tangled sleeping-bag into the centre of the room when a black dog appeared in the doorway and began barking furiously. Kent screamed at it and a man's voice almost immediately called, 'Winston!'

'Forget your bloody Winston,' shouted Kent Bailey at the top of his voice, 'my mate here has had an accident and he needs help.'

FOUR

Harry already had a show of spring flowers. He worked methodically on his knees tidying up the borders while Gary trundled a light mower across a lawn which was beginning to thicken, his left hand dressed and padded. Kent laboured to dig the heavy soil for planting. None of the three was talking but nobody noticed. The weather was mild and Gary had been allowed out of hospital for the afternoon. At last Harry laid down his trowel and slowly straightened up, rubbing his back and watching Gary working.

'Don't you go overdoing it now,' Harry called.

'What you worrying about him for?' panted Kent. 'Look after your own. I'm knackered.'

Harry grinned. 'You offered to do it.'

'Yeah,' returned his grandson. 'And the money'd better be good, I tell you.'

The old man reached for the tree near the corner of his caravan and drew himself upright. 'Right then,' he said. 'Tea for three?'

'And biscuits,' called Gary.

'Not forgetting the biscuits,' echoed Harry. He moved stiffly to the caravan door. Kent came to the end of a trench and helped Gary empty the cuttings into the compost box. They took a rest.

'All right then?'

'Yeah. You?'

'Not bad.'

Kent hated hospitals but in the five days since he had found Gary they talked in the ward obsessively. Nobody had ever taken his opinions seriously before and the pair became confessional about almost everything that mattered: parents, college, friends, sex.

The Bunker and the bullying were taboo subjects for the moment though both accepted there would be a need to talk them out when the friendship was strong enough. Gary's experiences with the YPF were another touchy subject in view of the prayer meeting at the Baileys' front door but Gary often talked about them which Kent thought hilarious.

'Love bloody love, right?' he said, lying back on a plastic sack and watching birds wheel in the sky. 'All that love. They wanted you to sing it, say it, pray for it, whatever. What they didn't like was anybody doing it.' He giggled.

Gary sat in the deck chair with closed eyes. Kent thought churches were morbid and Gary wasn't so sure any more that God existed. He hoped so because he needed him. But he'd find him in his own way. Jesus seemed the signpost but he wasn't entirely certain even of that. He knew he'd had enough of churches and people who wanted to mould you in their private image.

'Stop thinking!' shouted Kent. 'You're doing it again!'

Gary opened his eyes, grinning. 'How did you know?'

'Never you mind. What time you got to be back in hospital?'

'Five. Mum and Dad are picking me up here.'

Kent rolled over and began picking stones from the freshly turned soil. 'Any news when you're going home?' He spoke carefully. This was another difficult topic.

Gary shook his head. Bellings Brewery had cancelled Derek's tenancy of The Lion and would pay some compensation but not much. Derek called it less a golden handshake than a tin two-fingers. The Byrnes would be leaving The Lion.

'Tea's up, my lads,' called Harry, carrying the battered tin tray towards the boys. With a grin Kent hauled Gary protesting from the depths of the canvas chair. The old man carefully laid tea and biscuits on the upturned box they used as a table and looked round in contentment. He had the feeling there could be good times.

Gary walked over to help himself to a couple of biscuits and glanced round at Kent. The boy's lean body was taut with concentration and his eyes locked on a sparrow preening on the tree near the caravan. His arm slid back like a sling, his fingers making tiny automatic adjustments to the stone in his hand.

'You want your tea?' shouted Gary loudly. The bird fluttered away and Kent swung round, annoyed. 'You what?' he said. His eyes gleamed briefly. 'You what?'

Alick Rowe

VOICES OF DANGER

It is 1916, two years into the Great War. Alex Davies and Seb Carpenter are 16-year-old Cathedral choristers – until Alex is faced with the threat of expulsion. The two boys enlist under age and are sent to the Somme. After surviving a surprise German raid on Pave, the two boys rejoin their original platoon in the trenches where a new shock awaits them . . .

"utterly authentic . . . gripping and terrifying without being overdone . . ." *Robert Westall*

"This poignant story of betrayal will strengthen [Alick Rowe's] reputation as an author of high calibre."
The Sunday Correspondent